## Two Hearts in Hungary

Aletha knew instinctively that the Prince wished to kiss her.

Then, as she glanced at the Prince, she knew he was reading her thoughts.

For a moment they just looked at each other.

"I suppose you know," he said, "you are torturing me unbearably! The sooner you go back to England the better!"

He spoke so violently that Aletha stared at him in astonishment.

Without speaking another word he turned his horse and galloped back to the Palace . . .

### *A Camfield Novel of Love by Barbara Cartland*

———

*"Barbara Cartland's novels are all distinguished by their intelligence, good sense, and good nature...."*
—ROMANTIC TIMES

*"Who could give better advice on how to keep your romance going strong than the world's most famous romance novelist, Barbara Cartland?"*
—THE STAR

Camfield Place,
Hatfield
Hertfordshire,
England

Dearest Reader,

Camfield Novels of Love mark a very exciting era of my books with Jove. They have already published nearly two hundred of my titles since they became my first publisher in America, and now all my original paperback romances in the future will be published exclusively by them.

As you already know, Camfield Place in Hertfordshire is my home, which originally existed in 1275, but was rebuilt in 1867 by the grandfather of Beatrix Potter.

It was here in this lovely house, with the best view in the county, that she wrote *The Tale of Peter Rabbit*. Mr. McGregor's garden is exactly as she described it. The door in the wall that the fat little rabbit could not squeeze underneath and the goldfish pool where the white cat sat twitching its tail are still there.

I had Camfield Place blessed when I came here in 1950 and was so happy with my husband until he died, and now with my children and grandchildren, that I know the atmosphere is filled with love and we have all been very lucky.

It is easy here to write of love and I know you will enjoy the Camfield Novels of Love. Their plots are definitely exciting and the covers very romantic. They come to you, like all my books, with love.

Bless you,

# CAMFIELD NOVELS OF LOVE

## by Barbara Cartland

A New Camfield Novel of Love by

# BARBARA CARTLAND

## Two Hearts in Hungary

JOVE BOOKS, NEW YORK

TWO HEARTS IN HUNGARY

A Jove Book / published by arrangement with
the author

PRINTING HISTORY
Jove edition / November 1991

ISBN: 0-515-10712-3

Jove Books are published by The Berkley Publishing Group,
200 Madison Avenue, New York, New York 10016.
The name "JOVE" and the "J" logo
are trademarks belonging to Jove Publications, Inc.

PRINTED IN THE UNITED STATES OF AMERICA

10  9  8  7  6  5  4  3  2  1

# Author's Note

WHEN I visited Budapest at Easter in 1987, I found it one of the most beautiful cities in Europe.

At the same time, everything was very different from when the Empress Elizabeth of Austria found it the joy and delight of her heart.

During the Revolution, as is inevitable, much of the inside of the Palace had been gutted, but it has now become a Museum.

The Karolyi Palace was pulled down in 1933 and a great number of the old houses have been lost.

Although there appeared to be no poverty, I was aware of the constrictions that being behind the Iron Curtain imposed on the Hungarians, who have always loved to be free.

As I was driving along beside the Danube with

exquisitely beautiful views on each side of the road I asked:

"Where are the horses? It seems extra-ordinary to come to Hungary and not see horses!"

"You are now in the Holiday Area," I was informed, "and you have just left the City, which is the Business Area. The next area is Agricultural, and after that, a long way away, you will be able to see some of our horses."

I can imagine nothing could be more frustrating to a Hungarian, when horses have always been as much a part of his life as his family.

When I left Hungary my passport was inspected three times at the Airport by soldiers wearing large pistols at their belts.

I can only assume that they were ensuring that I was not a Hungarian trying to escape!

## chapter one

# 1878

LADY Aletha Ling ran into the house, across the hall, and into the Breakfast Room.

She knew she was late, but it had been such a wonderful morning.

She had therefore ridden for longer than she intended.

As she entered the room, her father, the Duke of Buclington, looked up, and she said quickly:

"I am sorry to be late, Papa. Do forgive me, but it was so lovely in the sunshine that I forgot the time."

Her father smiled, and Aletha saw with relief that he was not annoyed.

In fact, he looked very pleased and she wondered what was the reason.

She helped herself from the side-table on which stood a row of entrée dishes.

They contained fish, sausages, kidneys, eggs, and fresh mushrooms.

Then, as she sat down at the table, her father said:

"I have received some very good news!"

"Good news, Papa? From whom?"

"As it happens, from the Empress of Austria!"

Aletha put down her fork and exclaimed:

"Do you mean she has accepted your invitation?"

"She has," the Duke said with satisfaction. "Her Majesty is coming here for a week before she goes to Cottesbrook Park in Northamptonshire."

Aletha gave an exclamation before she said:

"So she is going to hunt with the Pytchley."

"She is," the Duke said, "and undoubtedly Earl Spencer will be delighted!"

Aletha was remembering that two years earlier the Empress Elizabeth had rented Easton Neston at Towcester.

She had wanted to hunt with the famous Bicester and the Duke of Grafton's hounds.

To say she caused a sensation was to put it mildly.

The English had not believed the stories of her horsemanship, thinking that anyone as beautiful as the Empress would be only a "Park-Rider."

In fact, it was whispered that the two picked horsemen, Colonel Hunt and Captain Bay Middleton, who were instructed to give Elizabeth a lead, were not very pleased about the assignment.

"What is an Empress to me?" Captain Middleton asked the Duke. "I will do it, but I would rather be on my own."

He took back his words the moment he met the Empress.

Himself one of the best riders in England, he recognised her brilliance on a horse as well as her incomparable beauty as a woman.

He had fallen deeply in love.

Young though she was at the time, Aletha had the idea that her father also had lost his heart to the irresistible Empress.

The Duke, too, was an outstanding rider.

After the Empress had returned to Austria, she had invited him to stay with her.

He had returned admiring her even more than he had when she was in England.

Aletha guessed that he had been very eager that his invitation to Ling Park should be accepted.

The tension of waiting had certainly made him somewhat disagreeable these last weeks.

But now at last the reply had arrived.

"I am so glad for you, Papa," Aletha said, "and it will be very exciting for me to meet the Empress."

Two years earlier she had been only sixteen.

She had therefore not been asked to any of the parties which were given for the Empress.

Nor had she been able to go out hunting with her father.

She had, in fact, been at School the whole time the Empress was in England.

When Aletha returned to Ling for Christmas, everybody, including the Duke, was still talking about the Empress.

She could understand that the Empress had become his ideal woman.

He had been very lonely after her mother died.

Aletha suspected there were quite a number of women only too willing to try to make him happy.

But he had busied himself with his estates, his horses and, of course, his daughter.

There was no doubt that the Duke loved Aletha and he hated being parted from her.

He had sent her to a Finishing School simply because it was the right thing to do.

Only now, when she was about to make her debut, was she able to be with him day after day, as they both wanted.

The Duke had his own pack of hounds.

Aletha, as she ate her breakfast, guessed that he was thinking what were the best days' hunting they would be able to give their distinguished guest.

Then suddenly the Duke put down the letter he had been holding in his hand and said:

"I know what I must do! I cannot imagine why I did not think of it before!"

"What is that, Papa?" Aletha asked.

"When she stayed at Easton Neston, the Empress brought her entire stable from Hungary."

"I had no idea of that, Papa."

"We want more horses—of course we want more horses," the Duke said, "and I will buy them in Hungary."

Aletha's eyes lit up.

"That is what I have always wanted you to have, Papa," she cried. "Besides, the Empress loves Hungary more than any place in the world, and the horses she rides come from there."

"She may *ride* them," the Duke said, "but we are going to *hunt* them, and I am determined to have the very best."

"But of course," Aletha agreed.

She knew her father's stable was already full of superb horses and his racing-stable was outstanding.

At the same time, there was always room for more.

She herself had always longed to ride the fiery, swift Hungarian horses that had captured the imagination of Europe.

"If you are going to Hungary, then of course, Papa, you must take me with you," Aletha said.

The Duke sighed.

"I wish I could do that," he said, "but you know I have to leave next week for Denmark."

Aletha gave a cry.

"I had forgotten that! Oh, Papa, must you go?"

"How can I refuse?" the Duke asked. "I am to represent Her Majesty, and she was talking to me about it only two days ago."

"It would be much more fun to go to Hungary!" Aletha said.

"I agree with you," her father replied. "But it is impossible, so Heywood will have to go for me."

James Heywood was the Duke's Manager, but in a rather different relationship than was usual for men in that position.

To begin with, he was a gentleman.

Secondly, he had been outstandingly brilliant as an amateur rider, winning a great number of races on his own horses.

Unfortunately, he had lost almost all his money through bad speculation.

He was therefore forced to work for his living rather than just enjoy himself by riding.

It was the Duke's father who had realised Heywood's capabilities and had employed him nearly twenty years before.

James Heywood was getting on to be an elderly

man, but his eye for a horse was still as keen as it had ever been.

The Duke, who was always extremely busy, had trusted him to buy most of the horses he possessed.

"Yes, Heywood must certainly go," he said as if he were thinking aloud. "We shall want eight or ten outstanding horses besides those we already possess."

"I suppose we shall have time to train them to the English countryside," Aletha questioned, "and to acclimatise them by the Autumn?"

Her father smiled.

"Shall I say we will do our damnedest!" he replied. "I shall look forward to the Empress's delight when she sees what we have provided for her."

There was a look in her father's eyes when he spoke of the Empress which Aletha recognised.

She wished now as she had wished before that he could find somebody to take the place of her mother.

She knew that she personally would feel jealous because she wanted him to herself, but she longed for him to be happy.

The Duke was still a very handsome and attractive man.

He had married young and his son, who was now twenty-three, had been born the following year.

Because his wife was not strong, there was a gap of five years before Aletha arrived.

The Duke had not yet reached his fiftieth birthday.

As he was extremely athletic, he had the figure of a young man, even though there were a few grey hairs at his temples.

"It will be lovely for Papa to have the Empress here," Aletha told herself unselfishly.

However, she could not help thinking it very sad that she and her father could not go to Hungary together.

It would certainly have been an adventure, and one she would have greatly enjoyed.

She understood, however, that he could not refuse to do what the Queen required of him.

After that, the Season would be in full swing.

There would be a thousand Social events in which the Duke would be involved.

Also as a débutante she was to have a Ball in London and be presented at Buckingham Palace.

"I must get in touch with Heywood at once," the Duke was saying. "Is he here or is he at Newmarket?"

Aletha thought for a moment.

"I am almost sure he is here, Papa. I saw him two days ago, and I know he is going to Newmarket next week."

"Then I will send for him—send for him immediately!" the Duke said. "What are we waiting for?"

He rang the gold bell which stood on the table beside his elbow.

The door was opened.

As was traditional, the servants were not in the room during breakfast.

Bellew, the Butler, appeared almost instantly, and the Duke said:

"Send a groom as quickly as you can for Mr. Heywood!"

"Very good, Your Grace!"

He responded to the urgency in the Duke's voice

7

by moving from the room more quickly than he usually did.

As he left, the Duke said:

"I am just wondering if we should have the 'Queen's Suite' redecorated?"

"I think it is unnecessary, Papa," Aletha replied. "You had it done two years ago for Princess Alexandra, and also the rooms occupied by the Prince of Wales. They have hardly been used since."

"I suppose not," the Duke agreed, "and we both know that all the Empress will be interested in is our stables."

He spoke complacently.

They were both aware that the stables at Ling were outstanding and the envy of every other Landowner in the County.

"This will certainly delight our huntsmen," the Duke went on. "They have been rather downcast recently by being overshadowed by the Bicester, and they will certainly be piqued that this year the Empress has chosen the Pytchley."

"That will give them an excellent reason for polishing themselves up," Aletha said, "and I will need a new riding-habit!"

"I suppose from Busvine, the most expensive Tailor in London!" The Duke smiled.

"Of course, and you, Papa, will need some new boots from Maxwell."

"I hate new boots!" the Duke complained. "My old ones are very comfortable."

"They are not smart enough," Aletha insisted.

She got up from the table as she spoke and kissed her father's cheek.

*8*

"I am so glad for your sake, Papa, that the Empress is coming. I know it will make you happy, and all the smart gentlemen in London who give themselves airs will be green with envy!"

The Duke laughed.

"You flatter me! You know as well as I do, my dearest, that the Empress is coming for the horses—not for me!"

"Now you are being mock-modest, Papa," Aletha teased, "and it is well-known that the Empress loves handsome men! A little bird told me that when you were in Vienna she danced with you every night, and many more times than she danced with anybody else."

"I cannot imagine from where you get all this non-sensical gossip!" the Duke complained.

But he was obviously pleased with himself.

Aletha thought it would be impossible for any woman not to find him attractive.

Later in the day the Duke told Aletha what instructions he had given to Mr. Heywood.

As he did so, she was regretting even more that her father could not go to Hungary and take her there with him.

She had read about the beauty of Budapest and the wonders of the Steppes where the horses galloped.

She had also heard of magnificent Palaces built by the Hungarian aristocrats.

They, she had been told, were the most handsome and attractive men in Europe.

If this was true, she could understand why the Empress preferred the Hungarians to the rather prosaic and stolid Austrians.

In fact, everyone knew she was very unhappy in Austria and felt free and unrestrained only when she was in Hungary.

The magnetism of the country drew her.

But there were also stories of handsome, hard-riding men.

They told her in words that were poetical and as beautiful as the country itself how much they loved her.

Aletha was very innocent.

She had not yet learnt of the *affaires de coeur* which were common in London amongst the Marlborough House set following the example of the Prince of Wales.

She had always been interested in the stories of the Empress of Austria and her overwhelming beauty.

She had therefore learnt a great deal about her simply by listening to her father's guests.

Of course the servants also talked incessantly about the Empress after she had visited England.

The gossip of the Servants' Hall was something Aletha's mother, if she had been alive, would have disapproved of her daughter hearing.

In 1874 the Empress had visited the Duke of Rutland at Belvoir Castle and hunted for the first time on English soil.

One of the housemaids from the Castle was now employed at Ling.

Emily, for that was the girl's name, talked of nothing but the beauty of the Empress, and Aletha learned a great deal from her.

Also, although he did not mean to gossip, from her father.

"The Queen, accompanied by John Brown," she heard him say to one of their guests, "called at Ventnor, where the Empress had taken a house."

"I hear she was there," the Earl replied, "because her daughter was ill, and sea-bathing was thought to be good for her."

"That is right," the Duke agreed. "But I am told that John Brown, of all people, was dazzled by the Empress's beauty!"

There was a great deal of laughter at this.

Aletha knew it was because John Brown was a rather dour Scottish gillie who was attached to Queen Victoria.

Because he was Her Majesty's favourite, he was often rude to the Courtiers and Statesmen in a way they resented.

When the laughter subsided, the Duke's guest said:

"John Brown may have been bowled over, but little Valeria was terrified of the Queen. In fact, she said: 'I have never seen such a fat lady!' "

There was more laughter, but Aletha, listening to the conversation, was interested only in what was said about the beautiful Empress.

There was a great deal more gossip when she came to England again two years earlier.

Then, needless to say, everybody talked about her association with Captain Bay Middleton, and the fact that the Empress was always in high spirits and quite untiring.

She had attended every Steeple-Chase in the neighbourhood, and after one competition had awarded a silver cup.

It was then that people began to speculate as to

whether it was the hunt or the man with whom she was hunting that made her seem more beautiful than she had been before.

Aletha had met Captain Middleton with her father.

She could therefore understand why the Empress admired him so much.

He was thirty, tall, and good-looking with red-brown hair and a dark complexion.

He was called "Bay" after the famous horse of that name which had won the Derby in 1836. Bay Middleton had been invited to Godollo for the hunting, and so was Aletha's father.

Aletha had prayed at the time that one day she might go with him.

Now the Empress was actually coming to Ling!

She knew nothing could be more thrilling for her father, herself, and everybody in the house and on the Estate.

There was no doubt that Mr. Heywood was excited when he heard the news.

"I was going to talk to Your Grace," he said to the Duke, "about some horses that are coming up for sale at Tattersall's this week. But if we are to buy Hungarian bloodstock, it will be unnecessary."

"Why do we not have both?" the Duke asked. "And if you leave for Hungary at the same time as I go to Denmark, there will still be time to have them in perfect trim by the time the Empress arrives."

"You know there is nothing I would enjoy more, Your Grace, than spending your money!" Mr. Heywood remarked.

The Duke laughed.

News of the Empress's proposed visit in the Autumn ran like wildfire through the house, the Estate, the villages, and the County.

On the following days there were endless callers.

They had really come just to ask if it was true that the Empress intended to stay at Ling.

"It is quite true," Aletha said over and over again.

She waited to see the surprise, excitement, and expression of envy which sprang to the callers' eyes.

Despite her assurance that nothing needed doing to the Suite the Empress would occupy, her father had already given orders that some improvements should be made.

The gold leaf on the ceilings and dados was to be touched up.

"How long are you going to be in Denmark, Papa?" Aletha asked when he began to arrange for his things to be packed.

His medals and decorations also had to be taken from the safe.

"I am afraid it will be at least two weeks, my dearest," he answered. "I wish I could take you with me."

"I wish you could," Aletha said. "It will be very dull here without you."

"Your Cousin Jane is coming to stay," the Duke replied.

Aletha made a little grimace, but she did not say anything.

Cousin Jane was over sixty and slightly deaf.

She lived only a few miles away, and was only too willing to come to Ling to chaperon Aletha whenever she was asked to do so.

At the same time, she was undoubtedly a bore.

Aletha knew that her father was careful not to have Cousin Jane to stay when he was at home.

However, there was one consolation.

She could escape from listening to Cousin Jane's constant complaints about her health by going riding.

Aletha had once suggested another and younger relative should chaperon her, but found she was a very bad horsewoman.

She became very resentful if those who were riding with her went ahead, leaving her behind.

It was not the same as having her father there to ride with her.

Whenever he was at home there were amusing people turning up to see him day after day.

There were also Point-to-Points and Steeple-Chases which took place in the vicinity.

"Do not be away too long, Papa!" she begged.

"Not one minute more than I have to," the Duke replied. "Much as I like the Danes, I find the ceremonial visits and the endless speeches that go with them extremely boring!"

"Surely the Queen could find somebody else to send in your place?" Aletha suggested crossly.

The Duke's eyes twinkled.

"Her Majesty likes to be represented by someone who looks the part!"

Aletha laughed.

"Which you certainly do, Papa! In fact, I suspect that as usual you will leave behind you a great number of broken hearts, and this time it will be Danish ones!"

"I cannot think where you get these ideas!" her father replied.

At the same time, she knew he rather enjoyed the compliment.

The day before the Duke left, Mr. Heywood arrived for a last word about the horses, before he too left the next morning for Hungary on his mission for the Duke.

They talked about horses all the afternoon.

Finally Mr. Heywood stayed for dinner, sending a groom to his house so that he could change into his evening-clothes.

When Aletha came down wearing one of the pretty new gowns which had been bought for her début in London, he said:

"You will undoubtedly, Lady Aletha, be the Belle of every Ball you attend, just as I remember your mother being many years ago!"

"I shall never be as lovely as Mama," Aletha answered, "but I will certainly do my best not to disgrace Papa as his only daughter."

"You will never do that!" Mr. Heywood replied.

He spoke with a sincerity she liked.

She knew he admired her, and it was somehow very consoling.

She was always afraid she would not live up to the reputation of the beautiful Lings, who all down the centuries had been acclaimed for their beauty.

They had been painted by every famous artist of their time.

In the Van Dyck Gallery at Ling there were portraits to which she bore a recognisable resemblance.

Also to those by Gainsborough, Sir Joshua Reynolds, and Romney, which hung in the Drawing-Rooms or on the stairs.

'I am certainly up against some very stiff competition!' Aletha thought.

Yet she knew that if Mr. Heywood admired her she need not be as nervous as she had been two or three years earlier.

Then she had gone through what she always referred to as her "ugly stage."

She was very conscious that her father's friends had said:

"Oh, is this Aletha? I always expected she would look like her mother, who I thought was one of the loveliest people I had ever seen."

They had not meant to be unkind.

At the same time, Aletha had prayed every night that she would grow more beautiful.

Then, almost like a miracle, her prayers had been answered.

Now she could definitely see, when she looked in her mirror, a distinct resemblance to her mother and to the other beautiful Duchesses.

But she was still apprehensive.

Later in the evening, when Mr. Heywood had gone, Aletha said to her father:

"I hope, Papa, Mr. Heywood is right, and when I appear in London, people will admire me."

"What you mean by 'people' is men!" the Duke said. "I can assure you, my darling, that you are very lovely now, and will be even more so as you grow older."

"Do you really . . . mean that . . . Papa?"

"I do," the Duke answered, "and I am already looking round to find you a husband."

Aletha stiffened and stared at him in astonishment.

"A . . . h-husband?" she stammered.

"Of course," the Duke said. "If your mother were here, I know she would be as eager as I am that you should make a brilliant marriage, and with somebody we would welcome as a son-in-law."

Aletha was silent for a moment.

Then she said in a small voice:

"I think . . . Papa, I would . . . rather find . . . my own husband."

The Duke shook his head.

"That is impossible!"

"But . . . why?" Aletha asked.

"Because in Royal and noble families like ours, marriages are always arranged discreetly but definitely."

He paused before he added:

"As my only daughter, I shall be very particular as to whom you will marry, and determined it will be somebody who will, in common parlance, 'fit in.' "

"But Papa, suppose I do not . . . love him?"

"Love usually comes after marriage, and I promise you, my precious daughter, I will find you a man with whom I am quite certain you will fall in love."

"B-but . . . suppose," Aletha said in a small voice, "he does not . . . fall in love with me and . . . wants me only because I am . . . your daughter?"

Her father made a little gesture with his hand.

"That, I am afraid, is inevitable. A man, if he is an aristocrat, of course hopes he will fall in love in the same way as I fell in love with your mother."

It was as if he were looking back in time before he went on:

"But he usually accepts what the French call a

*'mariage de convenance'* simply because 'blue blood' should be matched with 'blue blood,' especially if his bride is beautiful enough to carry on the line in the way that it should be."

Aletha was silent.

Then she said:

"I think that sounds very cold-blooded, and rather like being a piece of goods on the counter of a shop."

"It is not really like that," her father said a little sharply. "I promise you, my dearest, I will not make you marry anyone you do not like."

"I want to . . . love someone," Aletha said softly, "and I want him to . . . love me for . . . myself."

"A great many men will love you for yourself, but when it is a question of marriage, I think I am far more likely to choose the right man to ensure your future happiness than anyone you could choose for yourself at your age."

"What do you mean by that?" Aletha asked.

"I mean," the Duke replied, "that a young girl is easily deceived by a man who has the 'gift of the gab,' as it is called."

He thought before he went on:

"Honeyed words do not always come easily from somebody who is self-controlled and has been brought up not to 'wear his heart on his sleeve!' "

"What you are inferring," Aletha said slowly, "is that I might be carried away by what a man says to me and not by what he is feeling."

"There are men who can be very glib," the Duke said cynically, "especially when it is a question of money and rank."

Aletha was silent.

She knew that any man in England, whoever he was, would consider it a privilege to be the son-in-law of the Duke of Buclington.

She was the Duke's only daughter.

While the major part of his fortune would go to her brother, who at the moment was in India as *Aide-de-Camp* to the Viceroy, some of it would be hers.

She had also been left a considerable sum of money by her mother.

Her father had not put this into words.

She was, however, intelligent enough to realise there would be fortune-hunters in London who would consider it a great triumph if they could marry her.

It would not be for herself, but, as he had said, as her father's daughter.

"We have not really had a chance to talk of this before," her father was saying, "but I had intended to do so before we go to London."

He paused a moment and then went on:

"My dearest, you have to be sensible and leave things in my hands. You have trusted me since you were a child, and I cannot believe that you will not do so now."

"I love you, Papa, and of course I trust you," Aletha said. "But I want to fall in love as you fell in love with Mama, and she with you."

"That is something that happens only once in a million years!" the Duke replied. "When I walked into the room and saw your mother, there seemed to be a dazzling light about her, and I knew that I had found the girl—whoever she might be and from wherever she came—that I wanted as my wife!"

"And Mama said," Aletha replied, "that when she

saw you she knew you were the man of her dreams."

"We were very, very happy," the Duke said.

There was a pain in his voice that was always there when he spoke of his wife.

"I too want to feel like that," Aletha said quickly. "I want to meet the . . . Prince of my . . . Dreams!"

"Then you must just pray that is what you will do," the Duke replied.

She knew as he spoke that he did not believe it was possible.

As he said, what had happened to her mother and him was something that might happen once in a million years.

The Duke rose to his feet.

"If I am to leave early, I think I should go to bed. Do not worry about anything, my precious, and we will talk about this when I come home and before we leave for London."

He put his arm around her before he added:

"Enjoy yourself with the horses. I promise I will make up to you for the two weeks of boredom as soon as I return."

"I shall miss you . . . Papa."

"As I shall miss you."

The Duke walked up the stairs with his arm round her shoulders.

When they reached her bedroom door, he kissed her affectionately.

As he went down the passage to his own room, the Duke was mulling over in his mind the young men he had seen recently at Court.

It was not easy to choose one who seemed to be suitable as a husband for his daughter.

There always seemed to be a flaw, something which told him instinctively that they would be unfaithful within twelve months of the Wedding Ceremony.

'I will find somebody,' he thought confidently as he got into bed.

*     *     *

Aletha having undressed, pulled back the curtains, and was looking out the window.

There was a full moon, and the stars filled the sky.

It was still cold at night, but the moon on the lake glimmered like silver.

The daffodils were just beginning to make a carpet of gold beneath the old oak trees.

Usually Aletha was very moved by the beauty of her home and everything about it.

Tonight, however, she was looking out with unseeing eyes.

She was thinking of leaving everything she loved and which was familiar to go away with a strange man to a strange house.

There would be strange servants instead of those who had known her since she was born.

There would be strange relatives who would doubtless disapprove of many of the things she did.

Perhaps the man she married would not ride as well as her father did, or, for that matter, as well as she rode herself.

"How can I bear it?" she asked. "And yet I want love . . . the love which will make everything . . . even a cottage . . . seem wonderful because . . . he is there."

She found herself thinking of the Empress Elizabeth.

*21*

Because of her beauty, so many men loved her, and, if gossip was true, there were some she loved in return.

Aletha knew she wanted something very different for herself.

She wanted marriage in which the outside world did not matter.

A marriage where the only thing that counted was her love for her husband and his love for her.

She looked at the moon.

"Am I asking the impossible?" she enquired. "Must I really be content with 'second best'?"

She knew that love after marriage would never be the same as marrying the man of her dreams.

Would horses, however magnificent, however swift, however exciting, be the same as love?

She wished that this topic of conversation had not arisen the night before her father was to leave for Denmark.

She wanted to go on talking to him.

She wanted to try to make him understand that while she was perhaps asking the impossible, she must nevertheless strive to find it.

She suddenly had a terrifying feeling.

Suppose, almost before she could realise what was happening, she found herself the wife of some strange man with whom she had very little in common?

"I cannot bear it!" she said aloud.

She thought that if that should happen, she would run away.

Her father was going to Denmark.

Perhaps in Denmark he would find her a husband, a foreigner, a man whose language was different and about whose national customs she knew nothing.

She felt a sudden panic sweep over her.

It was almost as if she had been sailing on a smooth sea which had suddenly become tempestuous.

'I must escape!' she thought.

Then she told herself she must be sensible, talk to her father and explain to him how she felt.

Because he loved her, he would understand.

She had an impulse to run to his room, to tell him now what she was feeling.

She wanted to know that he understood, as he had understood when as a child she was frightened of the dark.

Then again she told herself that would be a very selfish thing to do.

He had to leave early in the morning to cross the North Sea to Denmark.

"Why does he have to go now—at this moment?" she asked angrily.

Instead, they could have been setting off together from Tilbury to Ostend and travelling from there by train to Budapest.

Together they could have inspected the Hungarian horses.

They would have ridden side by side in the strange, wild country, which was the joy and delight of the Empress.

"If we were there, it would be easy to talk to Papa about love," Aletha told herself.

But it was Mr. Heywood who was going to Hungary instead of them.

It would be he who would have all the fun of selecting the finest horses.

It was something she knew she would enjoy more than anything she had ever done, especially if she could be with her father.

She could imagine how excited they would be at finding really superb animals which were exactly what they wanted.

It was exasperating to think that everything had gone wrong.

She turned from the window.

It was no use wishing for the moon.

She had to stay at home and worry about the future.

It was certainly something she could not talk about to Cousin Jane.

Impulsively she turned again to the window to look up at the stars.

"Let me . . . find a man I will . . . love . . . and who . . . will love . . . me."

It was half a wish and half a prayer, and she felt as if it flew up into the sky.

Perhaps, she thought, there really was a "man in the moon" who was listening to her.

Then, as she put up her hand to draw the curtains and shut out the night, she had an idea.

It was so extraordinary, so incredible, that for a moment she was still.

Then something strong and defiant rose like a flame within her.

It seemed to seep through her body and into her brain.

She looked up once again at the moon, as if that were from where the idea had come.

"I will . . . do it," she said softly, "but you will . . . have to . . . help me!"

## chapter two

ALETHA had very little time in which to carry out what she planned to do.

In fact, she took two or three hours to pack her clothes, which she had seldom done herself.

She had also to decide how she could obtain enough ready money with which to travel.

As was to be expected, she had only a small amount of cash in her handbag, mainly to use in Church.

It was also there in case she had to tip somebody unexpectedly when she was out riding.

She knew, however, she would need quite a considerable sum for the journey she had in mind.

There was only one solution, and that was the jewellery which she had inherited from her mother.

Because she loved it, she had been allowed to wear some of the pieces since she left School.

So she kept a number of the brooches and bracelets

in the drawer of her dressing-table.

The tiaras, the necklaces, and the ear-rings were all in the safe.

These she could not obtain without alerting the Butler.

He would undoubtedly think it very strange that she should want jewellery in the middle of the night.

She therefore looked through the brooches she had inherited.

There was a diamond crescent brooch which had been too big for her at her age to wear.

She knew the stones were good and therefore it was valuable.

She put it into her handbag.

Then she remembered somewhat belatedly that she would need her passport.

She had one of her own because soon after her mother died her father had thought it would be a good idea for them to have a change of environment.

He had taken her to France to stay with the *Comte* de Soissons, who was an ardent race-horse owner like himself.

Before leaving, the Duke had anticipated that he might have to return to England at the request of the Queen.

He had therefore arranged for Aletha to have her own passport instead of just being included on his.

It was a letter signed by the Marquess of Salisbury, who was Secretary of State for Foreign Affairs.

It was fortunate there was no way of identifying the holder except that she was in possession of the pass-port herself, for Aletha had already decided that once she was on foreign soil she would use a false name.

It was unlikely when she had reached Hungary that her passport would be looked at except by officials.

Then she thought of what she was intending to do.

She knew it was outrageous.

When her father learned of it he would undoubtedly be infuriated.

At the same time, she told herself, unless she was unlucky, she would be able to return home before he did.

Then there would be no reason why he should suspect that she had not been staying with one of her friends.

Cousin Jane had arrived at six o'clock that evening and had fortunately gone straight to bed.

Consequently her father had asked Mr. Heywood to dinner, so that they could go on talking about horses.

Aletha was delighted that they had all escaped from a boring meal with Cousin Jane mouthing banalities or else discussing her health.

It was in fact her health that had solved Aletha's problem.

Her Lady's-Maid had come to Aletha to say:

"I am afraid, M'Lady, my mistress isn't well. She's got a very bad cold and as it's infectious I've put her straight to bed."

"That was very sensible of you," Aletha replied. "I certainly have no wish to catch a cold at the moment."

"She'll be better in a day or so," the maid said confidently, "and Her Ladyship always likes staying at Ling."

Aletha gave a sigh of relief.

Now she knew she could put her plan into operation.

When she finished packing she sat down and wrote a note to Cousin Jane.

She said that as she was ill she was going to visit some friends for a few days.

She also left a letter for her father just in case he should return before she did.

Because she loved him she told him the truth.

He would be angry, but at the same time with any luck his anger would have abated by the time she did return.

She looked at the clock.

She had finished everything she had to do, and could now rest.

She planned to leave as soon as she dared after her father had gone.

It was four miles to the Railway Station, and she knew he was leaving at six o'clock.

She also knew from their conversation at dinner that Mr. Heywood had arranged to travel to London with her father on the same early train.

He would reach London in time to catch the Steamer to Copenhagen which left shortly before mid-day.

If he missed it, there would be a delay of two days.

That would certainly upset the programme that had been planned for him in Denmark.

Because Aletha was so excited and at the same time nervous of what she was doing, she was unable to sleep.

She lit a candle every hour to see the time.

When it was six o'clock she heard her father walking down the corridor towards the stairs.

She could also hear the footsteps of his Valet and of the footmen carrying down his luggage.

He had been very insistent that she should not see him off.

"I want you to sleep until your usual hour, my dearest," he said, "and also, if I am honest, I am rather disagreeable first thing in the morning, and I do not want you to think of me like that when I am away."

"I could never think of you in any way except with love," Aletha assured him, "and that you are the most wonderful man in the world!"

Her father kissed her.

"You are a good girl," he said, "and I am very proud of you. I am quite certain Heywood is right and you will take London by storm."

"I hope so, Papa," Aletha replied.

Now as she heard him leaving she wondered if he would be so angry with her.

If so, he might refuse to allow her to make her début.

Then she knew that if he did so it would cause a scandal.

So she was quite certain that when she did return, her escapade would be hushed up and nobody told about it.

"I will get back before Papa in any case," she decided, "and I am sure I can swear Mr. Heywood to secrecy."

When she knew her father had left the house, she got up and dressed.

She was taking a considerable amount of luggage, including her hunting-boots and riding-habits, besides, of course, her pretty new gowns and her smart bonnets.

There was just a chance that she might meet some of the exciting Hungarian aristocrats.

If so, she was determined to look her best.

At a quarter past six she went from her bedroom, dressed in a travelling-cloak.

To her rather plain bonnet she had fixed a veil which had belonged to her mother.

Only married women wore a veil, and she thought it would be an effective disguise.

She did not intend to reveal herself to Mr. Heywood until fully committed to the journey.

Meanwhile she would appear to be an older woman who could be travelling alone.

This was actually a hazard.

When Aletha had come back from France without her father she had been escorted by an elderly Lady's-Maid and a Courier.

It was he who arranged everything for her.

He was there as a protection from the moment she left the French Château until she was back at Ling.

But she was determined that nothing, however difficult, would prevent her from reaching Hungary.

As she came down the stairs two night-footmen were still on duty.

They and two other footmen who had been there to see her father off looked at her in surprise.

She ordered two of them to collect the luggage from her bedroom.

Another was told to run to the stables and say she required a carriage to take her to the Station.

"Because we were so preoccupied last night with His Grace," she said, "I forgot to tell anyone that I too am leaving this morning to stay with friends."

She knew this would be repeated throughout the house when it was discovered she had gone.

The carriage came round to the front-door surprisingly quickly.

The Duke always became extremely irritable if he had to wait when he wished to go anywhere.

The grooms were therefore used to saddling a horse or putting a pair between the shafts in what was record time.

Aletha's luggage was piled into the carriage.

Only as the footman opened the door for her did he ask:

"Be ye goin' alone, M'Lady?"

"It is such a short distance," Aletha replied with a smile, "that it was not worth my taking a maid with me."

The footman shut the door and they drove off.

As she reached the Station she expected to have a long wait until the next train came in.

In fact, it was only fifteen minutes before one appeared.

The Porter, who knew who she was, found her an empty First-Class compartment, and put a label on the window marked RESERVED.

As the train moved off, Aletha thought with satisfaction that she was safely over the first hurdle.

But she had to be very sensible when she reached London.

She had time to plan exactly what she should do.

The train steamed past fields green with young crops and woods where the trees were just coming into leaf.

By the time they reached the suburbs, Aletha had everything planned in her mind.

She knew she could not afford to make any mistakes or miss the ship that was sailing from Tilbury at one o'clock.

A Porter found her a Hackney Carriage, and having tipped him before he shut the door, Aletha said:

"Tell the driver to go to the nearest Pawnbroker's. It must not be too far out of our way because I have to catch a Steamer at Tilbury."

The Porter looked at her in surprise.

Then he said rather familiarly:

"Come wivout yer money, 'ave ye?"

"Yes, I have," Aletha replied. "I was stupid enough to leave it on my dressing-table, so unless I am to miss the ship to Ostend, I have to pawn my brooch!"

The Porter grinned.

"That'll teach yer t'be a bit more careful next time, Ma'am!"

"It certainly will," Aletha agreed.

The Porter gave the instructions to the Cabby, who appeared to understand.

He whipped up his horse and they drove off.

When they stopped at the Pawnbroker's, Aletha was relieved to see that it had a respectable-looking shop-window.

It was in a comparatively quiet street.

She got out of the carriage.

Feeling nervous, although she did not show it,

she was pleased to see that the shop was empty of customers.

An elderly man with a large hooked nose was behind the counter.

"Good-day," she said.

Holding out her diamond brooch, she went on:

"I would like to pawn this for a very short time because I unfortunately left my money at home and have to catch a Steamer to Ostend."

It was the excuse the Porter had put into her mind.

"When'll you be back?" the man asked in a somewhat aggressive tone.

"In ten days," Aletha said firmly. "I promise you I have no wish to lose my beautiful brooch, but I cannot travel with no money in my purse."

The man turned the brooch over in his hand, examining it very closely.

Then he said:

"I'll give you seventy pounds, an' I wants one hundred back when ye redeems it."

Knowing the value of her mother's diamonds, Aletha knew she was being cheated, but she was not prepared to argue about it.

"I will accept that," she said, "as long as you promise me that you will not sell it in the meantime. It belonged to my mother, and I could not bear to part with it for long."

The old man looked at her penetratingly, as if he was questioning whether or not she was speaking the truth.

Then, unexpectedly, he smiled.

"I believe ye," he said, "but another time don't be so careless! Young ladies o' your age shouldn't be patronising Pawnbrokers."

"It is something I have certainly never done before," Aletha said, "and thank you very much for helping me, but it is very important that I catch this particular ship."

The Pawnbroker opened a drawer which appeared to be full of money and counted out the seventy pounds very carefully.

He handed it to Aletha and she put it away in her handbag.

"If you're alone," he said in a fatherly manner, "you keep a tight 'old on that there 'andbag o' yours. There be thieves an' pick-pockets as'll 'ave it off ye."

"I will do that," Aletha answered.

"There be plenty o' thieves, I 'ears, on the ships," the Pawnbroker went on, "an' if they don't take it off a pretty girl at cards, they'll take it wiv kisses!"

The way he spoke made Aletha shiver.

He gave her a ticket by which she could redeem her brooch.

She put this too into her handbag which she tucked tightly under her arm.

Then she held out her hand.

"Thank you very much," she said. "I will remember your advice."

"You do that," he said, "an' if you ask me, you're too young t'be travellin' alone."

Aletha smiled at him.

But when she got back into the carriage she knew he was right.

She might encounter quite a lot of trouble until she gained the protection of Mr. Heywood.

She knew however that it would be a terrible mistake for him to see her before they were in the train from Ostend.

It was an express which would take them first to Vienna.

She had heard him discussing the journey with her father, although she had not listened very attentively at the time.

It had not occurred to her then that she might do anything so outrageous as to join him.

When the idea had come to her the previous night, she had felt it was something she had to do.

Why should she stay at home and listen to Cousin Jane croaking over her illnesses?

She should have been travelling with her father to Hungary to buy the horses with which to delight the Empress.

She could not accompany him, but why not Mr. Heywood?

The moment she began to think about it, everything seemed to fall into place like a jig-saw puzzle.

She had to be sure that Mr. Heywood could not make her return home like a piece of unwanted luggage.

It would be impossible once they were in the train on their way to Austria.

They arrived at the Dock and she saw the Steamer waiting.

It was getting on towards one o'clock, and there were quite a number of people going up the gangway.

Mercifully there was no sign of Mr. Heywood, and she hoped that he had already embarked.

Then she felt with a sudden panic that she might at the last moment find there was no accommodation for her.

She pulled her veil down over her face.

Because of what the Pawnbroker had said, she put on a pair of spectacles that her father had used when he had visited Switzerland one year.

He had bought them out there and when he got back to England he explained:

"The sun was so brilliant on the snow that it hurt my eyes. The Swiss Ambassador suggested I should wear these slightly tinted spectacles."

Aletha had not thought of them again until she was just leaving the house.

Then she remembered the spectacles were in a drawer in a chest which contained dog-leads and riding-gloves.

She had slipped them into her handbag before she ran down the steps to get into the carriage.

She felt now as if they protected her from the world; also if Mr. Heywood did happen to see her, he would be most unlikely to recognise her.

She thought the Cabby looked at her in surprise.

She certainly appeared somewhat different from the way she had when he had picked her up.

She found a Porter to carry her luggage and went ahead of him up the gangway.

Having travelled with her father, she knew that not having a reservation meant she had to go to the Purser's Office.

There were several people ahead of her.

When finally it was her turn, she asked if it was possible to book a cabin.

36

To her relief there was one available.

She knew this was because the cabins were expensive and the majority of travellers were not prepared to spend extra money on them.

A steward brought her luggage into the cabin she had been allotted.

When he shut the door, Aletha thought with relief that she was now safe until they reached Ostend.

Having crossed the Channel to France with her father, she knew she was a good sailor.

Although the sea was slightly "choppy" with the wind churning the waves into "white horses," she did not feel in the least seasick.

Only when the Steamer was out of sight of the coast did she think with delight that she had taken her second hurdle in style.

"I have been clever," she told herself. "At the same time, I must not be seen by Mr. Heywood when we reach Ostend."

She guessed that like most men he would want to walk around the deck and enjoy the sea breeze.

The Courier had booked them the best cabin aboard the Steamer in which she had travelled with her father.

He had, however, "pooh-poohed" the idea of staying in it.

"I hate being shut up," he had said firmly.

He walked around the deck almost the entire time they had taken to cross from Dover to Calais.

As Aletha was hiding, she wanted to stay in her cabin for as long as possible.

Only when one of the stewards suggested he should take her luggage ashore did she come out.

Keeping her head low, she hurried down the gangway to walk the short distance to where the train for Vienna was waiting.

As she did not have a ticket, she had to buy it before she went aboard.

In a way it was a blessing, because it ensured that Mr. Heywood would have already taken his seat.

He would certainly not be looking particularly for anybody he might recognise.

The First-Class fare with a Sleeper was expensive.

Aletha thought it was a good thing she had been sensible enough to have plenty of money for the journey.

She knew of course that Mr. Heywood would have to pay for her return.

At the same time, in case anything went wrong she might have to look after herself.

It would be frightening to be in a foreign land and penniless.

At least she had her ticket.

The Porter discovered in which carriage her Sleeper was located and carried her luggage into it.

Aletha could speak French fluently.

She enquired from him how long it would be before the train stopped so that the passengers could eat at a Station Restaurant.

The Porter replied with all the information she required.

She realised that despite her spectacles and the veil which covered her face, he was looking at her with an undoubted look of admiration in his eyes.

"I must be careful," she told herself.

She certainly had no wish to be involved with any of the male passengers other than Mr. Heywood.

Ten minutes after she had boarded the train it began to move out of Ostend.

She had taken the third hurdle.

Now at least she felt safe from being sent home ignominiously.

The next difficulty would be to find Mr. Heywood.

There had been a great deal of talk in the newspapers about the introduction of coaches with corridors.

It would mean that the passengers could move from one compartment and from one coach to another.

Her father had disapproved of the idea.

"Men could frighten women by knocking on their doors and entering their compartments."

He paused a moment and then went on in a hard voice:

"It would also make it easier for thieves to rob a traveller when he was asleep."

"I saw in one newspaper," Aletha had replied, "that it might mean that a train that was going a long distance could have a Restaurant Car, and the passengers could walk down the corridors to it."

"Then one would have to eat while being shaken about by the movement of the train," her father replied, "which is something that women, at any rate, would dislike."

At the moment, however, Aletha thought it would have made it much easier for her to find Mr. Heywood.

As it was, she would have to wait until the train arrived at the Station, where they would disembark to have a meal.

She took off her bonnet and settled herself comfortably in her carriage.

At least she had one to herself.

She thought how uncomfortable it would have been if she had to travel with other people.

It would mean sitting up all night instead of being able to lie down.

She had read in the newspapers how comfortable Queen Victoria's private carriage was in which she travelled in France.

Her Majesty's Sitting-Room was connected with her bedroom and a luggage room in which her maid slept on a sofa.

Aletha thought that if she had been with her father, perhaps they would have been able to have a private coach.

It would have been very exciting.

'Nevertheless,' she told herself, 'I am on my way, and now I shall see the Hungarian horses that thrill the Empress, and will certainly please her when she comes to stay at Ling.'

Because she was interested in the land through which they were passing, she sat looking out the window.

She was quite surprised when she found the time had passed more quickly than she expected.

In fact, it was nearly six o'clock—the time at which the train was expected to stop.

She thought it would be a mistake not to wear her veil and spectacles until she found Mr. Heywood.

She therefore dressed herself carefully as she had been when she came aboard.

When she looked in the small mirror she thought that even her father would have found difficulty in recognising her.

With a great deal of smoke and even more noise the train steamed into a Station and came to a halt.

There were numerous people on the platform, and some of them were boarding the train, while others were meeting travellers from it.

There were also porters and trucks containing the Mail and a great deal of luggage.

Aletha waited a few minutes before she opened her carriage door.

She made sure that the steward in charge of her coach understood that she was leaving her possessions while she had dinner.

She thanked him in her excellent Parisian French when he told her he would take care of them.

Then she walked to the Restaurant.

It appeared to her when she first entered that every table was taken.

She could see no sign of Mr. Heywood.

She thought helplessly that she might have to return to the train without having anything to eat.

Then a man who was sitting at a table near to the door said to her in French:

"There is a seat here, *Madame*."

With a quick glance Aletha realised that beside the man who had spoken to her there was an elderly couple.

They looked, she thought, as if they might be Austrian.

A little reluctantly, still hoping she would see Mr. Heywood, she sat down in the empty seat.

"It is always difficult to find a place," the man said who had spoken to her before, "unless one jumps out of the train almost before it stops."

"I should have thought they might have enough places for everybody!" Aletha replied.

She spoke in a cold voice.

She felt by the way the stranger was smiling at her that he was not deceived by her disguise.

Because he was polite and there seemed no point in being rude, she allowed him to suggest what was palatable on the menu.

She knew a Frenchman would advise her better than anybody else.

She refused however when he asked if she would share his bottle of wine with him.

"No, thank you," she said firmly.

"You are making a mistake," he said. "You must know that in places like this it would be dangerous to drink the water."

He paused and smiled at her before continuing:

"What I have ordered comes from a famous Vineyard and is quite excellent!"

Because it seemed stupid to refuse, Aletha accepted a glass.

The food was not long in coming.

Yet while she was still eating, the elderly couple, having consumed little but drunk two huge mugs of beer, returned to the train.

"Now we can talk," the Frenchman said. "Tell me about yourself, because, I can see, *Mademoiselle,* that despite those disfiguring spectacles you are very pretty!"

Aletha stiffened.

She was about to reply that she was not a *Mademoiselle*.

Then she realised that although she had thought of

everything else, she had not remembered she should be wearing a wedding-ring.

The idea had not occurred to her when she had taken off her gloves to eat.

But the Frenchman had not missed the ringless fourth finger of her left hand.

As she did not reply, he bent a little nearer to her.

"Tell me about yourself," he said, "and may I say I find you very fascinating and intriguing."

"I am just a traveller, *Monsieur*," Aletha replied, "and as time is getting on, I am eager to get back to the train."

"It will not move for at least another twenty minutes," he replied, "and I want to know a great deal about you, and also you must tell me which coach you are in."

There was something in the way he spoke that made Aletha look at him sharply.

He put his hand out and took hers.

"I have not a Sleeper," he said. "I was unfortunately too late to obtain one, so why should you not be generous and share yours with me?"

Aletha tried to take her hand away, but he held on to it.

"We could both be very happy," he said softly, "on what is otherwise a very tedious and uneventful journey."

"The answer is 'No,' *Monsieur*, definitely 'No'!" Aletha said.

She meant to speak in a firm, crushing voice, but instead she only sounded very young and rather frightened.

The Frenchman's fingers tightened on hers.

"I will make you very happy," he said, "and when we are alone I will tell you how beautiful you are and how thrilled I am to have found you!"

There was a determination in his voice which frightened Aletha.

It flashed through her mind that if she went back to her carriage, he would follow her.

She might be unable to prevent him from entering her compartment.

Then she knew she would be at his mercy.

There would be nothing she could do about it.

She thought quickly that the only thing she could do was to appeal to the steward.

But the Frenchman might even be able to prevent her from doing that.

She felt her heart thumping in her breast, and a sense of panic swept over her.

The waiter came up for the bill, but the Frenchman did not loosen his hold on her hand.

He pulled two notes out of his pocket and gave them to the waiter.

"I would prefer to pay for myself!" Aletha said.

"I cannot allow you to do that," the Frenchman insisted.

She struggled to free her hand, but he still held it captive.

He took the change from the waiter, put it into his pocket, and rose to his feet, still holding on to her fingers.

She sat still, looking up at him, and now she was really frightened.

The people in the Restaurant were moving towards the train.

In a few minutes she would have to go back to her compartment.

The Frenchman began to pull her to her feet.

She tried to resist him, but it was hopeless.

Then, as he moved towards the door still holding her prisoner, she saw coming from the very back of the Restaurant a figure she recognised.

The Frenchman, dragging her as if she were a reluctant mule, had almost reached the door.

He had to wait for several people to pass, and as he did so Aletha saw Mr. Heywood coming nearer.

With a sudden twist of her hand she moved sharply away from the door.

It took the Frenchman by surprise.

She pushed past the passengers queueing up to go through the door and threw herself against Mr. Heywood.

"I have . . . found . . . you! I have . . . found you!" she cried.

Mr. Heywood stared at her in sheer astonishment before he exclaimed:

"Lady Aletha! What on earth are you doing here?"

"I am on . . . the train," she answered, "and . . . looking . . . for . . . you."

It was then, before she could say any more, that the Frenchman was beside her.

He took her by the arm, obviously having no idea that she had been speaking to Mr. Heywood.

"Come along," he said, "there is no escape, so do not run away from me again."

"Go away and leave me alone!" Aletha demanded.

She was conscious as she spoke that Mr. Heywood was taller and looked very much stronger than the

Frenchman, who was not a big man.

She took Mr. Heywood's arm.

As if he realised what was happening, he said in English:

"Who is this fellow? Is he bothering you?"

"Send him . . . away! Please . . . send him . . . away!" Aletha begged.

There was, however, no need for Mr. Heywood to say anything.

The Frenchman obviously understood what Aletha had said and realised he was defeated.

He turned, and pushing his way through the crowd, disappeared through the Restaurant door.

Aletha gave a sigh of relief.

"I . . . I was . . . frightened," she said in a small voice.

"Do you mean you are here alone?" Mr. Heywood asked. "I cannot understand . . ."

"I wanted to . . . come to Hungary with . . . you as Papa could not . . . take me," Aletha said, "and I . . . had no . . . trouble until . . . that Frenchman . . . talked to me."

"You must be crazy to do anything so outrageous!" Mr. Heywood said. "Have you a compartment to yourself?"

"I have . . . a Sleeper."

She realised he was frowning, and in fact looked extremely angry.

By this time they had reached the door of the Restaurant.

The passengers were all hurrying onto the train, and some of the doors had been slammed shut.

"Where is your compartment?" Mr. Heywood asked.

Aletha went towards it and he said:

"I will come and see you at the next stop. You are not to get out until I do so! Then I want a full explanation of what is going on!"

He stopped speaking a moment before he went on:

"I think, Lady Aletha, your father would be very angry if he knew you were here."

"I . . . I know that," Aletha agreed, "but I did so want to . . . come with . . . you and buy . . . the Hungarian horses for . . . the Empress."

"I have to think how I can send you back with somebody to protect you," Mr. Heywood said grimly.

"I will not go!" Aletha retorted. "And I have a splendid idea which I will tell you about when you have . . . time to . . . listen."

She knew by the expression on Mr. Heywood's face that this was not the right moment to appeal to him to help her.

By this time they had reached her compartment.

To her relief, the steward was standing beside it.

He was waiting to lock the door when she was inside.

She looked up at Mr. Heywood.

"I shall be quite . . . safe until you . . . find me at the . . . next stop," she assured him.

Mr. Heywood did not answer.

Instead, in what she realised was quite fluent French, but with a decided English accent, he told the steward that no one was to approach her compartment.

Then he tipped the man so generously that he was

overcome by what he had received.

Without saying any more to Aletha, Mr. Heywood turned and walked away towards his own compartment.

It was, she saw somewhat ironically, in the next coach to her own.

"*Bon soir, Madame!*" the steward said as he closed the door.

The bed had been made up while Aletha was in the Restaurant.

She sat down on it, feeling for the moment apprehensive that Mr. Heywood was so angry.

Then she told herself it was what she might have expected, but there was nothing he could do.

He could either take her home immediately, which would mean he could not buy the horses her father wanted, or else he would have to carry out the plan she had thought out so carefully.

As she undressed, she thought how lucky she had been to find him.

She had never anticipated that anybody would behave as the Frenchman had.

Now, as she thought about it, she could imagine it would be quite a clever way of getting a comfortable compartment without having to pay for it.

Perhaps, besides finding a pretty woman amusing, he was also a thief.

If she had been obliged to endure his presence, he might have taken her money and what jewellery she had with her.

She could understand why Mr. Heywood was horrified at the idea of her travelling alone.

'All the same, I am here,' she thought triumphantly, 'and it will be impossible for Mr. Heywood to send me back!'

She undressed and got into bed.

The vibration of the wheels soon soothed her to sleep.

\*     \*     \*

When Aletha awoke, it was morning.

She remembered the train would stop for breakfast and she had to be dressed by the time Mr. Heywood came to collect her.

She pulled up the blind.

The countryside through which they were passing was very beautiful.

There were high hills in the distance, forests and broad, shining rivers.

She wished she knew exactly where she was, and, what was more important, when they would reach Vienna.

She dressed herself, but now she removed her mother's veil from her bonnet.

She put the coloured spectacles away in one of her boxes.

The sun was shining and she thought she would not need the heavy cloak in which she had travelled yesterday.

Instead, she unpacked a short jacket which was trimmed with fur.

She knew, although she could see little of herself in the mirror, that she looked very smart.

She only hoped that Mr. Heywood would admire her as he had done before.

He might then not be so angry as he had been the night before.

Her gown, which was in the very latest fashion, was draped in the front and caught at the back into what was a very small bustle.

She knew that any woman on the Station would be aware that she was wearing a model which had originally come from Paris.

Then, as the train came slowly into the Station, she was still afraid.

Perhaps Mr. Heywood would be too angry at her escapade to think of anything but that she was her father's daughter.

She should have been properly and correctly chaperoned, besides having a Lady's-Maid and a Courier with her.

# chapter three

Mr. Heywood collected Aletha from her compartment.

They walked side by side and in silence towards the Restaurant.

When he had ordered coffee and two dishes of fresh fish, he said:

"Now, Lady Aletha, I want the truth, and the whole truth, as to why you are here."

"The truth is quite simple," Aletha replied. "If Papa had not had to go to Denmark, I would have come with him to Hungary."

She smiled at him tentatively before she went on:

"Instead of which I was left with Cousin Jane who, as usual, was ill, and I could not bear to miss all the fun."

"Your father had no idea of what you were doing, I presume?" Mr. Heywood said in an uncompromising manner.

"No, of course not. I waited until he had left the house, then took the next train to London and joined the ship at Tilbury."

Mr. Heywood tightened his lips.

"And you did not make yourself known to me for the simple reason that you knew I would have sent you back."

"Of course," Aletha agreed. "And now I do beg of you to make the best of the situation."

"Do you really think I can do that?" he asked in an irritated voice. "You know as well as I do that you have to be chaperoned, and God knows where we will find someone in Vienna, or anywhere else!"

"There will be no need for a chaperone," Aletha said quietly.

Mr. Heywood stared at her.

"What do you mean by that? You must be aware that as a débutante it could ruin your reputation forever if it was known where you were at this moment."

"No one is going to know that 'Lady Aletha Ling' is here, unless you tell them."

She spoke defiantly, and as Mr. Heywood stared at her she explained:

"You will be interested to know that I am in fact 'Miss Aletha Link' and your granddaughter!"

There was a stupefied silence, then unexpectedly Mr. Heywood laughed.

"I do not believe it!" he said. "I cannot be hearing this!"

"You must see," Aletha said, "that it is a very plausible explanation for my presence, and who is to know in Hungary whether you have a granddaughter

**52**

or not? Certainly no one will think of me as Papa's daughter."

"Did you really think up this ridiculous Fairy Tale yourself?" Mr. Heywood asked.

"It is not as ridiculous as you might think," Aletha answered defiantly. "You have been asked by the Duke of Buclington to buy him some horses. Who is to care whether you arrive with a wife, a daughter, or a granddaughter?"

She realised as she spoke that Mr. Heywood's eyes were twinkling.

She suddenly had the idea that despite his age, he was so good looking that he would not expect to be asked to be somebody's grandparent.

As if he knew what she was thinking, he said:

"You are certainly original, Lady Aletha!"

"*Aletha,*" Aletha corrected him. " 'Lady' Aletha will cease to exist as soon as we cross the frontier into Austria and then into Hungary."

"In other words," Mr. Heywood said, "you are using your own Passport."

"That is true," Aletha replied, "but if you think that dangerous, I am quite certain I can alter my name from 'Ling' to 'Link,' and change the word 'Lady' into 'Miss.' "

"I think that would be a mistake," Mr. Heywood said, "and we can only hope that the frontier officials will not be so impressed by you that they talk about your visit."

Aletha heard what he said with a lift of her heart.

She knew that he had accepted the position she had contrived for herself.

There was, in fact, little else he could do.

She leaned across the table which fortunately they had to themselves.

"Please let me enjoy myself with the horses," she said. "I cannot believe you will have to go to parties or spend much time with the owners."

While her father treated Mr. Heywood as a Gentleman, to foreigners he would be only a man the Duke of Buclington employed.

They would not expect to entertain him themselves, or invite him to meet their womenfolk.

"That is true," Mr. Heywood said to her surprise.

She was aware that once again he knew what she was thinking.

"At the same time," he went on, "you may find it slightly uncomfortable to be just my granddaughter and meet on equal terms people who will treat you very differently from what you are accustomed to."

"I am not interested in anything but the horses," Aletha replied, "and I want to visit Hungary more than any other place in the world!"

"I only hope you are not disappointed!" Mr. Heywood remarked dryly. "And do not forget that there will be a 'Day of Reckoning' when you return home."

"I am hoping to do that before Papa returns," Aletha said.

"And if you do not?" Mr. Heywood enquired.

"Then he will naturally be very angry," Aletha admitted. "At the same time, I am sure he will not want anyone to know of my escapade, because if it was talked about, it would certainly be damaging to my reputation."

Mr. Heywood laughed again.

"You are incorrigible!" he said. "But you have obviously thought out every detail. Quite frankly, I cannot think how I can send you home without coming with you myself."

"Without the horses?" Aletha exclaimed. "Think how upset Papa would be if he could not produce them as a surprise for the Empress!"

Mr. Heywood was silent as he continued to eat his breakfast.

Aletha knew that she had won her battle, or, rather, jumped her fourth hurdle.

She was very elated with herself.

When they were back on the train, Mr. Heywood came to her compartment, where the steward had put away the bed.

They sat down on the cushioned seat and he told Aletha about the next stop, where they would have luncheon.

There was so much more she wanted to ask him.

"How long are we staying in Vienna?" she enquired.

"Only one night," Mr. Heywood said. "Your father wanted me to see the Director of the Spanish Riding School, who uses a number of Hungarian horses as well as the Lippizaners."

"Oh, I do want to see them!" Aletha exclaimed.

"I think that would be a mistake," Mr. Heywood said. "The Director knows your father well, and if he saw you, he would undoubtedly mention you in the letter which he will write to His Grace, telling him how pleased he was to help me."

Aletha sighed.

"It seems such a wonderful chance."

"I know," Mr. Heywood agreed. "At the same time,

unless you are going to make things worse than they are already, you have to let me decide what is best for you."

Aletha smiled at him.

"All right, you win! And thank you for being much nicer about this than I deserve."

"I am only horrified," Mr. Heywood said, "that you have got yourself into a situation which may have far-reaching consequences."

"You mean I may not be allowed to be a conventional débutante!" Aletha said. "In that case, I shall just have to work in the stables at Ling and with the race-horses at Newmarket and everybody can forget about me."

"I think that is very unlikely," Mr. Heywood said. "Now, please, Lady Aletha, while we are travelling, remember you are a very beautiful young woman, and Hungarian men are very romantic and impressionable."

"That is what I have always heard," Aletha said.

"Then you must concentrate on the horses and not listen to anything that is said to you."

"Now you are being unkind," Aletha complained. "Of course I want the men I meet to think I am beautiful. I am not nearly as lovely as Mama, and I have always been afraid that no one would ever look at me."

"Your mother was the most beautiful person I have ever seen," Mr. Heywood said, "and I am sure she would be horrified at the way you are behaving now."

The way he spoke made Aletha glance at him in surprise.

Then impulsively, without thinking, she enquired:

"Were you in love with Mama?"

Mr. Heywood started.

"That is a question you should not ask me," he began.

Then he smiled.

"I think every man who came in contact with your mother loved her," he admitted. "She was not only beautiful, but she was so charming, so kind, and so very understanding. Everybody told her their troubles."

"Including me," Aletha said. "It would be much more exciting to make my début in London if Mama were with me instead of Grandmama."

She paused before she added in a low voice:

"She is always very disagreeable when her rheumatism hurts her."

"I am sure it will be much more enjoyable than you anticipate," Mr. Heywood said. "But you must understand for your mother's sake, as well as your father's, I have to protect you from getting into unpleasant situations such as you encountered last night."

"I never expected a perfect stranger to behave like that!" Aletha exclaimed. "If as he intended, he had forced his way into my compartment, he might have . . . tried to . . . kiss . . . me, and that . . . would have . . . been . . . horrible!"

Mr. Heywood thought he would have done a great deal more than that, but he had no intention of enlightening Aletha as to what might have happened.

"Forget him!" he said sharply. "It is something that will not occur again. But you understand that you must keep beside me, and not do things on your own."

"Very well, Grandpapa!" Aletha said mischievously.

* * *

They arrived in Vienna late in the evening and drove to a new Hotel.

Aletha learnt it had been opened only two years before.

It was certainly very impressive.

When Mr. Heywood changed the single room he had booked for a very luxurious Suite, she was delighted.

The Sacher Hotel had already a reputation not only for being the smartest Hotel in Vienna, but also for having the best food.

Aletha was hungry because she had not found what they were offered at the last stop very palatable.

When they went downstairs to the impressive Dining-Room, she looked around her with delight.

She had stayed in Hotels only once before, on her journey to France with her father.

Now she thought the tables with their lighted candles and the waiters scurrying about serving the well-dressed and elegant diners were very exciting.

She appreciated that Mr. Heywood in his evening-clothes looked almost as smart as her father would have.

She had put on a very pretty gown which she had never worn before.

They chose their dinner with care from a long and

elaborate menu, and Mr. Heywood ordered a bottle of wine.

"I suppose you are going to tell me that you are old enough to drink wine?" he remarked.

"Of course I am!" Aletha replied. "I am grown-up, and anyway, Mama always allowed me to have a little champagne at Christmas and on birthdays."

"I find it difficult to think of you as a grown-up young lady," Mr. Heywood commented. "I saw you first as a tiny baby, and you grew into an attractive little girl . . ."

"Then I went through a very plain period," Aletha said honestly. "I used to pray every night that I would be as beautiful as Mama."

"I am not going to tell you that your prayers were answered," Mr. Heywood said. "I will leave all those compliments to the young men with whom you will dance when you get to London."

As he spoke, Aletha remembered that one of them would be chosen by her father to be her husband.

The idea made her shudder.

She told herself that whatever Mr. Heywood or anyone else might say, she would enjoy this journey.

She was on her own.

She was not overshadowed by some strange man who had asked her to marry him just because she fitted in with his Family Tree.

As if Mr. Heywood wanted her to enjoy herself, he described to her what the world had been like when he was a young man.

He said that her mother had taken London by storm when she was a débutante.

Later she captured the hearts of everybody at Ling when she had married Aletha's father.

"Why did you never marry?" Aletha asked him towards the end of dinner.

She knew as she spoke that many women must have found him attractive.

As he did not answer, she added:

"Was it because of Mama?"

"Partly," Mr. Heywood admitted, "but when I was enjoying myself in London, I had no wish to tie myself down."

"All you wanted to do, according to Papa, was to win races. And that is what you did do!"

"I won quite a number on some exceptional horses," he said. "Then, as I expect you know, the crash came."

"How could you lose all your money?"

"Very easily," he replied, "but I do not want to talk about it."

"No, of course not," Aletha said sympathetically. "Go on with what you were telling me."

"It was then your grandfather offered me the job of looking after his Racing Stud, and when he died, I continued to be employed by your father."

Without his saying so, Aletha was aware that although he enjoyed his position, it hurt his pride to work for someone rather than being his own master.

"I am sure Mama understood how you felt," she said aloud.

"Your mother was always charming to me and, as I have already admitted, it would have been impossible for any man not to love her. At the same time, she was only aware of one man—your father."

"And Papa thought only of her," Aletha replied.

She paused before she added:

"That is why I am glad he likes being with the Empress."

"Of course," Mr. Heywood said, "and you and I have to find him such superb horses that they eclipse anything the Empress owns herself."

Aletha clapped her hands.

"That is exactly what we will do."

They left the Dining-Room.

When they reached their Sitting-Room, Mr. Heywood said he was going first thing in the morning to see the Director of the Spanish Riding School.

"You are to stay here," he commanded, "and not go out until I return!"

"I want to see something of Vienna before we leave," Aletha said.

"I am sure we will have time after luncheon," Mr. Heywood replied. "Our train does not leave for Budapest until ten o'clock."

"Promise you will hurry back, otherwise I shall feel so frustrated at being cooped up in the Hotel that I shall fly out of the window!" Aletha threatened.

"I promise I will not be long," Mr. Heywood laughed. "Good night, Aletha!"

It was the first time he had used her name without her title.

Aletha smiled before she said:

"You are the nicest and quite the handsomest grand-father anyone could wish for!"

"Now you are flattering me!" Mr. Heywood said. "And I am suspicious that you are trying in some underhand manner to get your own way about something."

Aletha laughed.

She thought as she went to her bedroom that at least she had succeeded in making him agree to everything she had suggested.

*       *       *

It was annoying for Aletha in the morning when she was up and dressed but had to stay in the Suite.

It was in the corner of the Hotel and she could look out the windows in two directions.

She could see clearly the people moving about in the streets.

Carriages drove by, and the sunshine made everything seem as if it had turned to gold.

She thought if she listened she would hear the music of Johann Strauss.

Small boys were continually whistling.

How could she be in Vienna and not hear the music which had electrified London as well as everywhere else?

She knew that soon she would be dancing to one of the famous Waltzes.

Once again she thought it might be with a man whom her father had already chosen for her as a husband.

Her eyes darkened.

"How can I make Papa understand that I will marry no one until I fall in love?" she asked.

There was no answer to this question.

Because once again her thoughts were depressed

and dismal, she gave a cry of delight when Mr. Heywood appeared.

She ran across the room towards him.

"You have found out what you wanted?"

"The Director has given me a letter," Mr. Heywood replied, "to the man in Budapest who looks after the Royal Stables."

"Do you think he will know where we will find the best and the most magnificent horses?" Aletha asked.

"I am sure of it!" Mr. Heywood replied. "And now, as you have been so good, we will drive in an open carriage through the streets of Vienna before we have luncheon."

Aletha had her bonnet ready.

As they went downstairs she felt as if her feet had wings.

There was a smart carriage drawn by two white horses waiting for them outside the Hotel.

They set off with Aletha enjoying everything she saw—the high buildings, the fountains, the bridges over the river, and finally the great Cathedral which was known as the "Stephansdom."

"Please can I go inside?" she asked Mr. Heywood.

"Of course," he answered.

He told the coachman to stop, and they walked into the wonderful old building in which the Viennese had worshipped for centuries.

Inside there was the scent of incense.

Aletha felt strongly the vibrations of faith.

Candles were flickering in every Chapel and in front of the images which stood against every pillar.

She felt the atmosphere was different from anything she had felt in any other Church.

Dropping to her knees, she meant to pray for her father.

Instead, she found herself praying fervently that she would find what she was seeking, that she would be married for herself and not because she was her father's daughter.

She went on praying with a fervency which came from her very soul.

Suddenly she knew in some strange way she could not explain that her prayers had been heard.

It was almost as if somebody, perhaps her mother, was telling her that all would be well.

She must not be pushed into a loveless marriage.

If she married, it would not be to some stranger who was not the "Prince of her Dreams."

When she rose to her feet she went up to the nearest image and putting a coin into the box in front of it, lit a candle.

Her mother had told her when she was quite small that if one lit a candle, it carried the prayer she made up into Heaven for as long as the candle remained alight.

Aletha chose the longest and most expensive candle.

Mr. Heywood was waiting for her at the end of the aisle.

When she joined him she had no idea that her face was radiant with a light that seemed to come from within herself.

Without thinking, just as she might have done with her father, she slipped her hand into his.

He led her out of the Stephansdom and into the street.

They returned to the Hotel in the carriage which was waiting outside.

* * *

The train which carried them from Vienna to Budapest was not as comfortable as the one in which they had travelled from Ostend.

Mr. Heywood arranged that they had adjacent compartments.

When he tipped the attendant heavily he became very attentive.

He made sure their beds were made up as comfortably as possible when they were having dinner.

This was at a Station they reached two hours after the train had started.

The food was not exciting. At the same time, it was edible.

After the excellent luncheon they had enjoyed at the Sacher, Aletha was not hungry.

She had also, before they left, had a slice of the famous Sacher cake.

It was made from a secret recipe known only to the Hotel.

It had been invented by one of the young Sacher sons when he was only sixteen.

Aletha thought it was the most delicious cake she had ever tasted.

Their dinner therefore was not really important and their real interest was the horses.

"What shall we do if we cannot find the ones you really want?" Aletha asked.

"There is no fear of that," Mr. Heywood replied.

"I am only afraid our task will be difficult because we shall want to buy hundreds rather than the eight or ten His Grace requires."

"If we tried them all out," Aletha remarked, "we would still be riding in Hungary when the Hunting Season begins!"

Mr. Heywood laughed.

"That is certainly a thought, and one which would certainly not please your father!"

"And it is so important," Aletha said, "that we get home before he does!"

"I hope for your sake we do!" Mr. Heywood replied.

They reached Budapest the next morning.

The moment she stepped from the Station, Aletha was entranced by the beauty of the City.

She thought that no place she had ever seen before had such a fairylike quality about it.

Even the City's Eastern Railway Station named the Keleri Pu, which was extremely magnificent, had something magical about it.

"Actually," Mr. Heywood told her, "Keleri Pu is one of the grandest Stations in Europe."

"It seems strange," Aletha said, "that people should exert themselves to build such enormous Stations. Perhaps it is because they are so impressed by trains."

"Of course they are," Mr. Heywood agreed. "And quite rightly. Think of the time it would have taken if we had had to come all this way from England by carriage!"

Aletha laughed.

"That is true!" she replied.

Then as they drove away from the Station she could only look at the great towers and Palaces.

There were also the houses which had an almost Moorish appearance.

The Churches were a mixture of Gothic and Baroque with Renaissance monuments and riches.

They drove up a winding road rising higher and higher.

"Where are we going?" Aletha asked.

"Before we even unpack," Mr. Heywood answered, "we are going to the Royal Palace to see the man to whom the Director of the Spanish Riding School gave me an introduction."

He pointed to where above there was an enormous building.

"It is certainly impressive!" Aletha remarked.

She could see a great many pillars and a huge dome silhouetted against the sky.

"Is there any chance of the Empress being here now?" Aletha asked hopefully.

Mr. Heywood shook his head, and she was disappointed.

When they reached the Palace she was extremely impressed with the huge terrace outside it.

There was a beautifully carved fountain and an enormous equestrian statue.

Mr. Heywood told her it was of Prince Eugene of Savoy.

He had fought the Turks at the end of the seventeenth century.

He looked very dashing on his plunging horse.

Aletha thought he was just how she expected a Hungarian to look.

From the terrace there was a panorama of the City with the Danube dividing it.

It was so lovely that Aletha did not mind when Mr. Heywood said:

"I suggest that you sit here while I go inside and see if I can find the gentleman I wish to consult."

As she did not answer, he said:

"You will be quite safe in the carriage."

There were sentries on either side of the door through which he disappeared.

Aletha sat looking in the opposite direction.

She thought that no view from any Palace could be more beautiful.

Then because she wanted to see it from the balustrade itself, she got out of the carriage.

She walked first to the beautiful fountain.

Its water was pouring iridescent over rocks and statues into a stone basin beneath it.

Then as she reached the balustrade to look down at the boats moving slowly on the Danube, she said involuntarily:

"Could anything be more beautiful?"

"That is what I was thinking!" a voice said.

She started, then saw that standing beside her was a young man.

He was handsome, and there was something dashing and different about him that made her sure he was Hungarian.

He spoke in English, but with just a faint accent.

As she looked up at him he said:

"I thought for a moment you must be one of the Sylphs from the Danube whom I have often been told about but have never seen."

Aletha laughed.

"That is what I would like to be," she said. "But

surely no Palace could have a more wonderful view than this, and no Palace could be more impressive!"

"We are very proud of our Palaces," the young man replied, "and even more so of our horses!"

"They are what I have really come to see," Aletha told him.

"But you will not find them in Budapest," the Hungarian said.

"No, I know," Aletha answered, "and my . . . my . . . g-grandfather is inside the Palace now, finding out where we must go to see the finest of them."

"Why are you so interested?" the young man asked.

Because he was inquisitive, Aletha remembered that she should not be talking to a stranger.

It might be indiscreet anyway to tell him too much, and perhaps a different story from what Mr. Heywood was telling.

Instead of answering, she looked down at the river below.

A boat, its sails unfurled, was moving majestically down the river.

"If I am too curious, you must forgive me," the Hungarian said, "but you must understand it is a surprise to find a Sylph who is English standing outside the Palace and saying she is looking for Hungarian horses."

It sounded so ridiculous that Aletha could not help laughing.

"It just happens to be true!" she said.

"Then I only hope you will not be disappointed," the Hungarian replied.

"I am quite sure that will not happen," Aletha answered.

She was about to say something more, when there was the sound of horses' hoofs and the turning of wheels.

The next moment a carriage appeared and swept up to the front of the Palace.

It was a very smart vehicle with a coachman and footman wearing an elaborate livery.

The bridles and accoutrements of the horses were all of gleaming silver.

Seated in the carriage was a woman holding a small sunshade over her head.

The Hungarian had turned round as the carriage approached.

Aletha did so too and was able to have a quick glance at the occupant of the carriage.

She was exceedingly smart, and also very beautiful.

She had dark flashing eyes.

The ostrich feathers on her bonnet fluttered in the breeze as she looked towards the Hungarian.

She raised an elegantly gloved hand in his direction.

It was a call for him to attend to her, and he bowed in response.

Then he said to Aletha:

"I hope one day I may have the pleasure of seeing you again. In the meantime, I know you will enjoy the horses of my country."

"I am sure I shall," Aletha replied.

He walked away and she felt sure he was very athletic and would certainly be a good rider.

As he reached the lady's carriage the footman

jumped down to open the door for him.

He stepped into it to sit beside the lady with the sunshade.

She gave him her hand and he kissed it.

As he did so, Aletha turned away, feeling she was somehow prying on something which did not concern her.

As the horses drove away she deliberately stared down at the boats on the river.

She did not turn round until the sound of the horses' hoofs could not longer be heard.

She had only to wait a little longer before Mr. Heywood returned.

He looked surprised when he saw she was not in the carriage.

He walked to where she was standing.

"Has he been able to help you?" Aletha asked eagerly as he joined her.

"I have exactly the information I wanted," he replied, "with an introduction to the man who is my *vis-à-vis* in each of the places we shall visit."

"That is splendid!" Aletha said excitedly. "Where are we going?"

"First of all," he said, "we are going to the Castle of Baron Otto von Sicardsburg."

Aletha raised her eye-brows.

"He sounds German."

"He is. He married a Hungarian Princess and is a very wealthy man."

"His horses are good?"

"I am assured they are superb," Mr. Heywood said, "and fortunately for us, as we have so little time, the Baron's Castle is not far from the Palace of the Estérházys, who also have some of the finest horses in the whole of Hungary."

Aletha smiles.

"Shall we go there at once?"

"As quickly as the train will carry us!" Mr. Heywood replied.

As they drove away from the Palace he said:

"I suppose you know you have broken all the rules in walking about in the precincts of the Palace without permission?"

"I never thought of it!" Aletha exclaimed.

"I wonder no one reproved you for the offence," Mr. Heywood remarked.

Aletha thought there had been no reproof from the Hungarian.

In fact, he had looked at her with an expression of admiration which she had never seen before in any man's eyes.

He was certainly very good-looking and exactly what she thought a Hungarian gentleman—or was it aristocrat?—would look like.

It somehow seemed appropriate that he should be accompanied by a beautiful woman and driven away in a smart carriage drawn by superb horses.

'If I was breaking the rules,' she thought, 'I am not surprised he came and spoke to me, since of course he was curious as to why I was there.'

She thought she would like to remember him because he had admired her and likened her to a Sylph.

The conversation she had with him was however certainly not something she would relate to Mr. Heywood.

# *chapter four*

THE train carried them from Budapest to Györ which was in the Province of Sopron.

They got out at Györ which was a fascinating old town with houses of every period, and some beautiful Churches.

Mr. Heywood hired a carriage which was to take them to the Castle there which was where the Baron Otto von Sicardsburg lived.

Aletha thought it was very exciting to be in the country.

She looked eagerly around her and naturally at the horses.

She saw quite a number of them in the fields, or turned out to grass.

She thought they were different from any horses her father possessed, and was sure they were just as spirited as they were reputed to be.

The Castle was some way out of Györ, but Mr. Heywood told her they were going in the right direction for their next call.

This was the Palace of Prince Józsel Estérházy.

"Tell me first about the Baron," she pleaded, "or I shall get the two families muddled."

"Prince Estérházy would not be complimented," Mr. Heywood said. "He is one of the most important aristocrats in Hungary and is very proud of his heritage."

"And the Baron?" Aletha prompted.

"From what I gather from my informant in the Palace," Mr. Heywood said, "he is not very well liked, but that might just be national prejudice."

"I would much rather be with a Hungarian in Hungary," Aletha said as she smiled.

"So would I," Mr. Heywood agreed. "I find the Germans difficult, especially when it comes to business."

"Then let us hope we shall not have to stay with him for long."

Aletha was however impressed as they drove up the long road after passing through some enormous gates and saw the Castle ahead of them.

It was quite different from an English Castle and yet it had an unmistakable charm.

It was obviously very old with arched windows which made it picturesque.

As they had gone uphill to reach it, there was a magnificent view over the countryside.

Aletha was certain it had been a fortress of defence in ancient times when Hungary was continually at war.

It had three large, square turrets with flat tops which was unusual, but when they entered the court-yard the later additions were elaborate and Baroque.

Mr. Heywood got out of the carriage to explain to the servant who answered the door why he had come.

The carriage was then instructed to drive to the back of the Castle where the stables were located.

Separate from them was a house which was of a very different period from the Castle itself.

It was here that Mr. Heywood presented his Letter of Introduction.

He and Aletha were immediately taken into a Sitting-Room where a middle-aged man greeted them.

His name was Hamoir Kovaks, and he informed them in flattering English that he was in charge of the Baron's horses.

Mr. Heywood discovered that he talked French far more fluently.

They conversed in that language while consuming glasses of Tokay which Aletha tasted for the first time.

She had always associated it with the romance of Hungary and thought it was delicious.

By the time Mr. Heywood had explained to Mr. Kovaks exactly what he required it was too late to see the horses that evening.

Instead, they were shown to their bedrooms where they changed for dinner and came down to find Mrs. Kovaks waiting for them.

She was a pleasant, rather stout woman who when she had been young must have been very pretty.

But she was obviously of a class that was accustomed to being subservient to the nobility and was shy of foreign guests.

It made conversation difficult and Aletha was glad when they retired to bed.

The next morning both she and Mr. Heywood were up very early and hurried to the stables before breakfast.

The actual stables were not in any way as good as those at Ling, but the horses were everything that Aletha expected them to be.

After a quick inspection they had breakfast, then with Mr. Kovaks to guide them rode into the open countryside.

Grooms followed, each leading horses, so that they could change mounts whenever they pleased.

It was thrilling for Aletha.

Yet when they turned for home she had the feeling, without his saying anything, that Mr. Heywood was a little disappointed.

This was confirmed when as they walked back to the house he said to her in a low voice:

"Good, but not good enough!"

"Do you think we shall find something better?" Aletha asked.

"I am sure we shall," he answered. "At the same time, there are more being brought here for us to try."

When they went back after luncheon there were about twenty fresh horses in the stable-yard.

As Aletha walked towards them eagerly, a man came from the direction of the Castle.

At one glance she realised that it was the Baron.

He certainly looked German, but he was younger

than she had expected and in a way good-looking.

He was very tall, over six foot, and he walked with an unmistakable swagger.

He greeted Mr. Heywood in a condescending manner.

"I hear you have come from the Duke of Buclington," he said, "and of course I shall be pleased to sell His Grace any horses that take your fancy."

As he spoke he looked at Aletha for the first time, and his eyes widened.

"Who is this?" he enquired.

"My granddaughter is travelling with me," Mr. Heywood explained in a somewhat repressed tone.

"Then she must certainly be mounted on one of my best horses!" the Baron said. "And I will accompany you on your ride in case, Kovaks, you are not describing the best points of my animals accurately."

It sounded almost rude, but Mr. Kovaks merely bowed his head and said deprecatingly: "I do my best, Master!"

"So I should hope," the Baron retorted.

He looked at Aletha.

"I will go to change," he said, "then I shall see with my own eyes if the way you ride is as beautiful as you look."

He was obviously paying her a compliment.

At the same time, there was something familiar in his voice which made Aletha raise her chin.

The Baron did not take long to change.

When he came back he made a terrible fuss as to which horse he should ride.

Then he complained that the girths were not tight enough or the stirrups were too short.

He was showing off his authority, and Aletha thought he was just the sort of man her father would dislike.

Finally on the Baron's instructions she and Mr. Heywood accompanied him while the grooms came behind with fresh horses.

Mr. Kovaks was left in the court-yard.

They rode over much the same ground they had covered earlier in the morning.

Then the Baron drew in his horse and suggested that Mr. Heywood should change to one of the other animals.

"There are some jumps over there," he said, pointing in the direction of them, "which I would like to see you take, and I am sure you will not be disappointed in the horse you are riding."

Mr. Heywood dismounted, and Aletha said to the Baron:

"May I jump them with my grandfather?"

"No," the Baron said firmly. "The jumps are high for a woman."

Aletha was about to argue, then thought it would be a mistake.

As soon as Mr. Heywood had ridden away the Baron drew his horses nearer to hers and said:

"And now, pretty lady, tell me about yourself."

He spoke in an ingratiating tone which made her nervous.

She touched her horse with her whip to make him move forward.

The Baron followed her and he said:

"You ride superbly, and you are very lovely! There are a lot of things I want to talk to you about."

He spoke good English but with a decided German accent.

"I am listening, Baron," Aletha said coldly.

She did not look at him, as she was watching Mr. Heywood riding towards the first jump.

He took it brilliantly and went on to the next.

"My wife is away," the Baron was saying, "and I find it very lonely in the Castle, which I want to show you. You will enjoy seeing it."

"I am sure it is very interesting," Aletha said, "but as we are here for such a short visit, I doubt if my grandfather will have time."

"As it is your grandfather who is buying the horses and not you," the Baron said, "I will take you round this afternoon."

Aletha opened her lips to protest.

Then she thought it would be dangerous to antagonise the Baron.

She decided she would ask Mr. Heywood to say she was indispensable to his judgement as to which horses he required.

"What is your name?" the Baron asked.

"Aletha," she replied without thinking.

"A lovely name," he said. "As lovely as your eyes, and of course your lips."

He had drawn nearer to her, and as he spoke he put out his gloved hand and laid it on hers.

"We are going to know each other very much better than we do at the moment," he said softly.

Again Aletha urged her horse from him.

Then on an impulse she rode at the jump Mr. Heywood had just taken.

She heard the Baron give a shout as she went,

but she pretended not to hear.

Her horse took the jump with some inches to spare, and she felt her heart beating with delight that she had been able to do it.

Mr. Heywood had disappeared into the distance over the third jump, and she followed him.

She took the second in style, but her horse nearly fell at the third.

She managed, however, to keep him on his feet and to remain seated.

She found Mr. Heywood just ahead of her.

She rode up to him and he asked:

"Why did you follow me? These jumps are difficult for you on a horse you have never ridden before."

"I am here, safe and sound!" Aletha said blithely. "As a matter of fact, I am running away from the Baron."

"What has he been saying to you?" Mr. Heywood asked.

"He was just paying me a lot of tiresome compliments," Aletha said evasively.

Mr. Heywood turned back the way they had come, but avoided the jumps.

"The whole trouble," he said, "is that you should not be here on this journey, and certainly not without a chaperone."

"I am perfectly all right as long as I am with you," Aletha said soothingly.

She felt she had made a mistake in telling him that the Baron had been familiar.

He might make up his mind to buy what horses were available here, then return home immediately.

"What do you intend to buy?" she asked to change

the subject. "I thought the horse you are riding took the first fence magnificently!"

"They certainly are outstanding," Mr. Heywood replied. "But I expect the Baron, knowing your father is a rich man, will ask an exorbitant sum."

When they reached the Baron he was all smiles.

"I have never seen the horses jump better!" he said. "But, of course, they had exceptionally good riders."

He was looking at Aletha as he spoke, and she was careful not to meet his eyes.

They tried two or three other horses, then when they returned to the stables the Baron insisted they should have luncheon with him at the Castle.

There was nothing Mr. Heywood could do but accept the invitation.

He knew it would be extremely embarrassing for Kovaks if he refused.

The Castle was undeniably impressive with enormous rooms with arched ceilings.

There were huge stone fireplaces in which a whole trunk of a tree could be burnt when it was cold.

The Banqueting Hall could have seated fifty people with ease.

Aletha felt as if they were like peas rattling in a pod, while the servants in elaborate liveries served them on silver plates.

The furniture however was heavy and not attractive.

The pictures that hung on the walls were not particularly interesting.

When they left the Dining-Room they moved into a Salon.

It was large and elaborately furnished but not in good taste.

The Baron left them for a moment, and when he came back he said:

"As I am alone here and greatly enjoy your company, I have given orders for your things to be moved from Kovaks' so that you will be my guests tonight."

He was obviously speaking to Aletha, and she saw Mr. Heywood's lips tighten.

He could hardly refuse to accept the Baron's invitation and said:

"You are very gracious. At the same time, you will understand that we have to leave you early tomorrow to visit Prince Józsel Estérházy's Stud."

"You will find nothing there that I cannot supply," the Baron said sharply.

"I am afraid the arrangements are already made," Mr. Heywood said, "but I would like to buy for His Grace four of the horses we rode today."

"I am sure the Duke will need more than that!" the Baron retorted.

"It is actually a question of price," Mr. Heywood said.

Because it was something in which she was not interested, Aletha rose from her chair and walked across the room to the window.

The panoramic view was breathtaking.

At the same time, she was uneasily conscious that while the Baron was talking to Mr. Heywood and obviously haggling over the price, his eyes were on her.

She could almost feel them boring into her back.

She wished ardently that they could leave this afternoon.

Then she told herself she was being needlessly apprehensive.

As long as Mr. Heywood was there, what could the Baron do other than pay her exaggerated compliments?

They returned to the stables.

The Baron insisted that there were a number of horses Mr. Heywood should try before he finally made up his mind.

He tried to persuade Aletha that she had ridden enough for one day.

He would like, he said, to show her the gardens of the Castle and later the Castle itself.

She, however, made it clear that her only interest was in riding.

As Mr. Heywood backed her up, the Baron's stratagems to get her alone were defeated.

Finally they went upstairs to dress for dinner.

The Baron showed them their rooms with a triumphant air, as if he expected them to be very impressed.

The rooms were large and furnished in Germanic taste which had a typical pomposity about it.

The Baron first showed Aletha into her room, then took Mr. Heywood a little farther down the corridor to his.

A maid was waiting for Aletha and her luggage had been unpacked.

A bath was brought to her room, and when she was dressed she was wondering if Mr. Heywood would call for her when there was a knock on the door.

The maid opened it.

He came in, speaking slowly so that the maid understood.

He told her he wished to speak to his granddaughter alone.

She went out, closing the door behind her, and Mr. Heywood walked towards Aletha.

She was standing, having just risen from the stool in front of the dressing-table.

"I am sorry about this," Mr. Heywood said in a low voice.

"You mean our having to stay in the Castle?"

"I mean having that German making eyes at you!"

"I am glad we are leaving here tomorrow," Aletha said, "and please, do not leave me alone with him."

"I will take good care of that," Mr. Heywood said, "but you understand that you must lock your door and make certain there is no other access to your bedroom."

Aletha looked at him in astonishment.

"You do not mean . . . you cannot imagine . . . he . . . ?"

"I would not trust him as far as I could see him!" Mr. Heywood said.

"But . . . I never thought . . . I never imagined that a . . . gentleman would . . ."

"I know, I know," Mr. Heywood said quietly, "but, as you are aware, you should not have come here without a chaperone."

"I have you," Aletha said.

"As he thinks I am nothing more than a Senior Servant," Mr. Heywood said, "I would not put it past him to drug my milk or have one of his servants give me a crack on the head!"

Aletha gave a little cry of horror.

"Now you are frightening me, and suppose somehow he comes to my room and tries to . . . kiss me?"

"I have an idea—if you will agree."

She looked up at him and he said:

"When you come up to bed, undress. Then as soon as your maid has left you, come to me. I am just two doors farther down the passage. I will make sure that no one can break in, and we will exchange rooms."

Aletha clasped her hands together.

"That is clever of you, but suppose he sees us doing that?"

"I have ascertained that he sleeps a little way away in the huge Master Suite which obviously inflates his ego."

"Then that is what we will do," Aletha said. "And please make sure that when he finds I am not here, he does not come to your room."

"If he manages to get in here thinking he will find me, I shall knock him down!" Mr. Heywood said. "I may be getting old, but I can still deal with bounders like him!"

There was a grim note in his voice which made Aletha say:

"Thank you, thank you, for being so wonderful! I am sorry to be such a nuisance."

Unexpectedly Mr. Heywood smiled.

"It is the penalty for being beautiful," he said, "and I hope you are taking to heart the lessons that this journey is teaching you."

"In future," Aletha said, "I shall encase myself in armour-plating and carry a stiletto!"

Mr. Heywood laughed.

"At least you have a sense of humour!" he said. "Now come along; let us face the music and look out for the pitfalls."

They walked down the stairs, and when they entered the Salon the Baron was waiting for them.

Aletha had to admit that he looked his best in evening-clothes, although she avoided his eyes.

He, however, gave her his arm to take her into dinner and it was something she could hardly refuse.

As they left the Salon he put his hand over hers and she felt the pressure of his fingers.

"You are driving me crazy!" he said in a low voice which only she could hear.

She did not answer, but looked straight ahead, carrying herself stiffly.

When they reached the Dining-Room the plates on which they were served were gold.

Magnificent goblets studded with precious stones ornamented the table.

The food was excellent, but rather heavy.

The Baron deliberately talked only to Aletha, ignoring Mr. Heywood as if he were not there.

He was quite perturbed that Aletha answered him in monosyllables.

He talked of his importance in Hungary, the advice he had given to the Emperor, and the house he was redecorating and restoring in Budapest.

Everything he said was egotistic and affected.

Aletha thought it would be impossible to find anyone more conceited or more pleased with himself.

They returned to the Salon.

She was just about to say she was tired and would like to go to bed when the Butler came into the room to say:

"*Herr* Kovaks wishes to speak to Mr. Heywood, *Herr* Baron."

"Perhaps it could wait until tomorrow," Mr. Heywood suggested.

"*Herr* Kovaks is in the hall, *Mein Herr,* and says it is very important," the Butler replied.

Mr. Heywood knew enough Hungarian to understand, and reluctantly he got to his feet.

Aletha also rose.

"I know you will understand," she said to the Baron, "but I am very tired, and I would like now to go to bed."

"Of course you shall do that," the Baron agreed, "but first I have a small present for you which I will show you while your grandfather is talking to *Herr* Kovaks."

He went to a table on which there was a small package.

There was nothing Mr. Heywood could do but follow the Butler out of the room.

As the door shut behind him, the Baron said:

"You are very beautiful, Aletha, and this is the first of many presents I hope to give you."

"It is kind of you," Aletha answered, "but I . . . I do . . . I do . . . not really . . . want a present."

"Open it!" the Baron ordered.

She undid the ribbon and removed the tissue paper from a long thin velvet box.

She opened it and, to her astonishment, inside was a narrow bracelet set with diamonds.

She stared at it and the Baron said:

"Now you understand how much I want you, and I will tell you later how much you attract me."

Aletha gave a little gasp and shut the velvet box.

She replaced it on the table, saying:

"Thank you, but you will understand that if my mother were alive . . . she would not . . . allow me to accept such an . . . expensive gift from a man . . . especially one who is a comparative stranger."

The Baron merely smiled.

"I will not be a stranger for long, and I have a great deal more than a bracelet to offer you, my pretty one!"

He was very close to her, and Aletha felt his arm go round her waist.

Quickly she extricated herself.

Before he could prevent her, she ran across the room and reached the door.

"Good night, *Herr* Baron," she said, and went out into the Hall.

Mr. Heywood was in conversation with Mr. Kovaks.

Aletha was certain it was the Baron who had arranged that Mr. Heywood was forced to leave them alone.

He looked at her enquiringly as she hurried past him in the direction of the staircase.

"I am . . . going to bed . . . Grandpapa," she said.

He knew by the inflection in her voice that something unpleasant had occurred.

He took a step forward as if he would go with her, then changed his mind.

He continued to talk to Mr. Kovaks until the Baron came to join them.

\*    \*    \*

In her bedroom the maid helped Aletha undress.

She put on her nightgown.

Before she got into bed she saw that her negligée, which was very pretty, was lying on a chair.

Beneath the chair were the soft, heel-less slippers which would make no sound as she walked down the corridor.

She told the maid she wished to be called early.

When the woman had gone, she got out of bed to listen at the door.

She could hear voices and knew that Mr. Heywood and the Baron were coming upstairs together.

They were talking about horses.

She listened as they passed by.

Then, as she looked down, she realised there was no key in the lock.

She knew that Mr. Heywood had been right in guessing what the Baron intended.

She thought how horrible it would be if he touched her and if his lips tried to take possession of hers.

She was thankful that Mr. Heywood had warned her what might happen, otherwise she would never have had the slightest idea that anyone who was supposed to be a Nobleman would behave so disgracefully, especially towards a guest in his own house.

She found it difficult to wait until everything was quiet before she went to Mr. Heywood's room.

He would have been provided with one of the footmen as his Valet.

Aletha knew she must be sure he was alone before she went to his room.

She was also afraid she might encounter the night-footman, who would be quenching some of the sconces after everybody had retired to bed.

The minutes seemed to pass by like hours.

At last she heard two men talking in low voices as they passed her door.

She thought they would be the man who had valeted Mr. Heywood and also the Baron's Valet.

As soon as she could hear them no longer, she very cautiously opened the door and peeped out.

As she expected, the lights in the corridor had been dimmed.

The candles of every second sconce were extinguished.

She shut the door behind her, and moving like a startled fawn, ran down the corridor.

The door to Mr. Heywood's room was ajar, and as she rushed in he was standing waiting for her.

A long dark robe which he was wearing made him look very tall and, she thought, very protective.

She ran to his side, saying as she reached him:

"There is . . . no key in . . . my door!"

"It is what I might have expected," Mr. Heywood said angrily. "Well, there is a key here and I have made sure there is no other way into this room. Lock the door as soon as I have left."

"S-suppose he . . . does somehow get in?" Aletha insisted in a frightened voice.

"If he does, scream! I shall be listening for you," Mr. Heywood replied.

He smiled at her.

"I am used to sleeping with one eye open when I am attending to sick horses."

"Then I will scream very loudly!" Aletha promised.

Mr. Heywood put his hand on her shoulder.

"Do not worry," he said. "I will deal with the Baron, and we will leave first thing tomorrow morning."

"Thank you . . . thank . . . you!" Aletha said. "I

**90**

hope Papa never learns about this . . . but if he does . . . I know he . . . will be very grateful . . . to you."

Mr. Heywood was walking towards the door.

"Lock yourself in as soon as I am outside," he said softly.

Aletha did as she was told.

Then she got into the big bed which was the same size as the one she had been allotted.

Because she was frightened she did not blow out the candles.

She merely lay with her eyes shut, saying a prayer of gratitude because Mr. Heywood was so kind.

The Baron was repulsive!

This was certainly something she had not expected to find in Hungary.

The Hungarian she had met by the balustrade outside the Palace had been very different.

He had paid her compliments, but they had not revolted her in the way the Baron's had.

He had certainly looked at her with admiration when he called her a "Sylph."

But he had not seemed in any way over-familiar or frightening.

'I wonder if I shall ever see him again?' she asked herself wistfully.

Even if she never did, she had a feeling that his looks and his charm had somehow set a standard.

It would be by that that she would judge other men in the future, the men she was to meet in London, and the man who was to be her husband!

## chapter five

ALETHA had breakfast in her bedroom which she knew must have been arranged by Mr. Heywood.

Everything was packed.

When she came downstairs she found him waiting for her in the hall.

He did not speak, he merely guided her through the front-door.

Outside, there was a travelling-carriage drawn by four horses.

She guessed that Mr. Heywood had arranged this with Hamoir Kovaks.

She suspected it had nothing to do with the Baron.

She got into the carriage, and Mr. Heywood tipped the servants and followed her.

She realised it was not yet half-past eight and there was no sign of the Baron.

Only when they were down the drive could she no

longer repress her curiosity and asked:

"What . . . happened? Did you . . . have a scene with . . . him last . . . night?"

Mr. Heywood sat back comfortably against the padded seat.

"It was a good thing," he said, "that you obeyed me. As I expected, he came to your room and was very surprised to find me there."

"What happened?" Aletha asked breathlessly.

Mr. Heywood smiled.

"I wanted to knock him down and teach him not to behave in such a way again, but I thought it would be a mistake in case he talked about you, and somehow the story got back to England."

"Then . . . what did you do?" Aletha asked.

She could not help feeling a little disappointed that the Baron had not got his just deserts.

At the same time, she realised that Mr. Heywood was a much older man.

He might have been hurt if they had struck each other.

Mr. Heywood's eyes were twinkling as he said:

"I pretended to be asleep when the Baron came in! I woke up with a start when I saw him peering at me in surprise."

"I should think he was astonished!" Aletha murmured.

"I had left two candles burning," Mr. Heywood went on, "and when I saw him I exclaimed:

" 'Forgive me, *Herr* Baron, I fell asleep and forgot to blow out the candles. How clever of you to realise that was what I had done, and I can only apologise profusely for my carelessness!' "

Aletha laughed.

"That must have taken him aback!"

"It certainly did," Mr. Heywood said, "and after a moment he remarked:

" 'See it does not happen again!'

"He walked towards the door and then, as if he could not prevent himself from asking the question, he enquired:

" 'Why has your granddaughter changed her room?' "

"What was your answer to that?" Aletha enquired.

"I said, staring at him pointedly:

" 'She was frightened when she found there was no key in the lock. It must have been overlooked. But she had promised His Grace the Duke before we left England that she would always lock her door in Hotels and also houses in foreign countries. She would not wish him to think she had disobeyed his instructions!' "

Aletha laughed.

"What did the Baron say to that?"

"He murmured something," Mr. Heywood replied, "then went from the room."

He paused before he added:

"I made quite sure he went to his own apartments, and I left my door ajar all night so that I could hear if you were in any trouble."

"Oh, thank you . . . thank . . . you!" Aletha cried. "You have been so clever! As he is such a . . . horrid man, I wish you could have taught him a lesson! But it is much more diplomatic for us to leave without there being any unpleasantness."

"That is what I thought," Mr. Heywood agreed,

"and you do see that in future you must make quite sure there is a key in your door and lock it."

"I am sure this sort of thing would not happen in England!" Aletha said innocently.

There was a somewhat cynical twist to Mr. Heywood's lips, but he did not disillusion her.

Instead, he started to talk about the Palace they were going to visit.

"It will take us some time to get there," he said, "so we will have luncheon on the way and arrive early in the afternoon."

"Tell me more about the Estérházys," Aletha pleaded.

"The Palace was built in the eighteenth century," Mr. Heywood replied, "by Miklós Estérházy and it was called 'Magnificent' by his contemporaries."

"I am longing to see it," Aletha murmured.

"It was under his patronage," Mr. Heywood went on, "that it acquired European fame and his home became a 'Hungarian Versailles.' "

"How did he do that?" Aletha asked.

"Not only was the Palace beautiful, but imaginative festivities took place there and were attended by the Empress Maria-Thérèsa. But even that did not satisfy Estérházy."

"What else did he want?" Aletha asked.

"First he had his own Opera House built, and employed Franz Joseph Haydn as Conductor to his private Orchestra."

"How wonderful!"

"Then he added a Puppet Theatre, and every kind of entertainment which brought all the famous people in the world to Fertõd."

"I cannot wait to see it!" Aletha exclaimed.

"I doubt if it will be as sensational now as it was then," Mr. Heywood said, "and do not forget that we are concerned only with their horses."

"I will not forget that!"

She realised that Mr. Heywood was hesitating over something else he was about to say to her.

She waited a little apprehensively, wondering what it could be.

"You have come with me," Mr. Heywood began, "and you have also chosen to be my granddaughter. You must therefore not be surprised if you are treated differently from the way to which you are accustomed."

"Of course I understand that," Aletha said.

"I have always been told that the Hungarians are very conscious of their own importance," Mr. Heywood went on. "I do not want you to feel insulted when you are treated as I will be—as a paid servant in your father's employment."

"I understand that," Aletha said, "but if people had any intelligence, or should I say sensitivity, they would be aware the moment they met you that you are a gentleman, and I, if nothing else, am born a Lady."

She spoke fiercely, but Mr. Heywood merely laughed.

"People treat one another as what they believe them to be rather than what they appear to be, but you may be quite certain the horses will not be class-conscious!"

They both laughed, and Aletha settled down to enjoy the beauty of the countryside.

There were mountains, twisting rivers, and fields filled with wild flowers.

It made them appear like an oriental carpet of brilliant colours and indescribable beauty.

They had luncheon in a small village where the women were wearing national dress.

The food was plain but good.

Aletha began to forget the Baron and to enjoy the enchanted land she had always believed Hungary to be.

The peasants looked happy and sang as they worked.

"Of course the Empress loves being here," she said, "and as the Hungarians love beauty, it is not surprising that they love her!"

"*Adore* is the right word," Mr. Heywood corrected Aletha. "She comes here whenever she can escape from the protocol and dullness of the Court in Vienna."

"We must make her very happy when she comes to Ling," Aletha said softly.

"I am sure we will find exactly the horses we want at the Palace of the Estérházys," Mr. Heywood said confidently.

"Did you buy any of the Baron's horses?" Aletha asked.

"I bought two just to make Kovaks feel that he has not been a failure," Mr. Heywood replied.

"That was kind of you."

They reached Fertőd early in the afternoon.

As soon as Aletha saw the huge wrought-iron gates, then the exquisite Palace, she knew it was even more wonderful than she had expected.

The Palace had a square tower surmounting it which

was characteristic of Hungarian architecture.

There were oval-shaped windows and the brilliant carvings above each one were unique.

The statues on the roof and the pillars which supported the portico were all reminiscent of Louis XVI.

As he had done before, Mr. Heywood left her in the carriage while he presented his credentials inside the building.

Aletha was entranced by the beautifully laid out garden with three fountains and many statues.

There was colour everywhere—the flowers, the shrubs, the trees all appeared to be in blossom.

The sunshine made everything dance in front of her eyes.

It was as if she were watching a ballet taking place in some magical theatre.

As she looked back at the house she saw a man coming out through the front-door and supposed it was Mr. Heywood.

Then to her astonishment she saw it was the Hungarian who had spoken to her on the Terrace of the Royal Palace in Budapest.

He was obviously going riding and carried a whip in his hand.

His high top-hat was set at a jaunty angle on his dark head.

He looked casually at the carriage with its four horses before he saw Aletha.

For a moment he was still, as if in astonishment.

Then he walked towards her.

"Is it possible that it is you?" he asked. "Or am I dreaming?"

He was speaking in English and she replied:

"I told you I was looking for horses."

"Then you have come to see mine—or rather—my father's."

"I naturally had no idea they were yours!"

He looked at the empty seat beside her and asked: "Surely you are not alone?"

"No, my grandfather is inside the Palace, explaining to somebody why we are here."

"This is the most surprising and delightful thing that has ever happened!" the Hungarian said. "Suppose we start by your introducing yourself to me?"

For a moment Aletha forgot who she was pretending to be and said:

"I am Aletha Li—!"

She quickly amended it to "Link," having very nearly betrayed herself.

The Hungarian bowed.

"I am delighted to meet you, Miss Link," he said, his eyes twinkling, "and I am Miklós Estérházy, eldest son of Prince Józsel."

"I know I should curtsy," Aletha remarked, "but it is rather difficult while I am sitting down!"

Prince Miklós laughed and opened the door of the carriage.

"Let us go to find your grandfather," he suggested, "and discover what is being arranged."

Aletha had the idea she ought to wait in case, as had happened at the Castle, they were driven to another house.

But the temptation to go inside the Palace was too great.

She stepped out of the carriage, Prince Miklós putting out his hand to help her.

They walked inside, and she saw at once that the interior was as beautiful as the outside.

The French influence was obvious and made everything look graceful rather than ponderous as it had been at the Baron's Castle.

They walked through the hall in which a number of footmen were in attendance and quite a long way down a passage.

"I think your grandfather will be with Héviz," Prince Miklós said, "who looks after our horses. He will doubtless be telling him how marvellous they are before he even has a chance to see them!"

As he spoke he opened a door.

They went into what Aletha thought was either a Secretary's room or an Estate Office.

There were maps all over the walls and a number of tin despatch boxes piled at one side.

The Prince was not mistaken.

Mr. Heywood was sitting in front of a desk where a man was talking in broken English and gesticulating with his hands.

Both men rose as they entered and Aletha said quickly to Mr. Heywood:

"I forgot to tell you, Grandpapa, that I spoke to Prince Miklós when I was waiting for you outside the Royal Palace."

She smiled at him as she went on:

"Of course I had no idea who he was, or that I would meet him here."

Mr. Heywood held out his hand.

"I am honoured to meet Your Highness!"

"And I am delighted that your desire for horses has brought you to Fertöd!"

He looked at the other man and added:

"I am sure, Héviz, you have already sold him a dozen before he has even seen them!"

"I hope so, Your Highness" was the reply.

"As I am going to the stables," the Prince said, "I suggest you and your granddaughter come with me."

"That is exactly what we would like to do, Your Highness," Mr. Heywood replied. "But I think first I must discuss where we are to stay, and must pay the carriage I hired to bring us here."

"If I had known, I would have met you at the Station," the Prince replied.

"Actually we came from the Castle at Györ," Mr. Heywood informed him.

"From Baron von Sicardsburg?" the Prince enquired. "He boasts a lot, but I can assure you, his horses in no way compare with ours. Is that not true, Héviz?"

"It certainly is, Your Highness!"

"He is a . . . horrid man!" Aletha said impulsively. "I am sorry we bought . . . anything from . . . him."

Prince Miklós gave her a sharp glance.

"You are quite right in what you say," he replied, "and you should have nothing to do with him."

"I hope . . . never to . . . see him . . . again," Aletha murmured.

Then she thought she was being indiscreet and looked towards the door.

"Do let us go to the stables," she begged.

The Prince turned to Mr. Heywood.

"You and your granddaughter must, of course, stay here," he said. "Is your name the same as hers?"

"No, Your Highness. My name is Heywood—

Aletha's mother was—my daughter."

He spoke in a way which told Aletha that he disliked having to tell a lie.

Because it also embarrassed her, she moved quickly towards the door.

The Prince was just in time to open it for her.

They walked ahead down the passage, followed by Mr. Heywood and *Herr* Héviz.

When they reached the hall, the Prince gave orders to the footmen to bring their luggage inside.

While Mr. Heywood was paying the coachman, the Prince took Aletha down a corridor.

"We can reach the stables quicker this way," he said, "and you can see a little of my home while we do so, although there is a great deal more I want to show you."

"I have already heard how magnificent it is," Aletha said, "and I would have been very upset if I had to go home without seeing the Music Room."

"So you also like music," the Prince said.

His voice deepened as he added:

"I have thought about you so much since I left Budapest. Have you thought of me?"

It was a question she had not expected and the colour came into Aletha's cheeks.

She knew she ought to say that she had forgotten him completely, but the lie would not come to her lips.

"You have!" the Prince said triumphantly when she did not answer. "I could not believe it was not on the order of the gods that we were brought together on the terrace of the Royal Palace."

"My g-grandfather said I had done . . . wrong in

getting . . . out of the carriage," Aletha said.

"I think you flew out of it," the Prince answered, "and because you are not human, no one saw you except me!"

Aletha laughed.

"I am quite prepared to believe everything is magical which happens in Hungary!"

"You like my country?"

"It is so beautiful that I can understand why the Empress loves it and longs to come here."

"So you have heard about our Empress!"

"Yes, of course, and that is why Papa . . ."

She bit back the words just in time.

She was going to say: "That is why Papa is buying horses for her to ride when she comes to stay."

Instead, tumbling over her words, she finished:

" . . . my g-grandfather is buying Hungarian horses for the Duke of Buclington."

"I had supposed they were for himself!" the Prince exclaimed.

"That is what he would like them to be," Aletha said, "for he was, when he was young, one of the best amateur riders in England, but he lost all his money."

"And are you saying that the Duke of Buclington now employs him?" the Prince enquired.

"Yes, that is right," Aletha said.

There was a little pause, and because she was aware of what the Prince was thinking, she said:

"I believe Your Highness had offered us the hospitality of your home under a false impression. If you wish to change your mind, my grandfather and I will, of course, understand."

"I have no intention of changing my mind," the Prince said quickly. "I only thought that your grandfather looked very much an English gentleman."

"That is exactly what he is!" Aletha said sharply.

The Prince looked at her, and she saw that he was smiling and his eyes were twinkling.

"Now you are accusing me," he said, "of a crime I have not committed. In fact, your grandfather looks so handsome with all the qualities we admire in an Englishman, I could not believe he was not rich as well."

Aletha had the feeling he was getting out of a rather uncomfortable situation very cleverly. Because she had no wish to quarrel with him, she smiled and said:

"I do feel that we are imposing on you, and I have already been told how proud and autocratic the Hungarian nobility are."

The Prince laughed.

"Now you are definitely trying to put me down a peg or two!" the Prince replied. "Please, my beautiful Sylph, do not be unkind to me!"

He spoke so beguilingly that Aletha felt she could say no more.

A moment later they were joined by Mr. Heywood and the Hungarian.

The stables certainly deserved the same description as the Palace—"Magnificent."

They were very different in every way from those which were owned by the Baron.

As they went from stall to stall, Aletha had eyes only for the horses and she knew they had found exactly what her father wanted.

Each horse seemed to be superior to the last.

When they had inspected at least two dozen, she looked at Mr. Heywood and said:

"Shall we make an offer for them all?"

"You will do nothing of the sort!" the Prince remarked before Mr. Heywood could reply. "These horses are all far too precious for us to part with them, and how can you be so cruel as to suggest that I should walk rather than ride?"

"I know our arrival has kept you from riding," Aletha said, "but if we change very quickly, could we please ride with you?"

"How long will you take to change?" the Prince asked.

"Two minutes!" Aletha replied, and he laughed.

"I will allow you eight more," he said, "and after that we will go off without you!"

Aletha gave a little cry of horror, and it was *Herr* Héviz who said:

"I will take you to your room. I am sure one of the maids will have unpacked for you."

They went back to the Palace and *Herr* Héviz had difficulty in keeping up with Aletha.

She almost ran down the corridor and up the very impressive staircase.

A footman had alerted the Housekeeper.

Aletha was taken to a very magnificent bedroom.

She was sure she would not have been given it if the Prince had not thought Mr. Heywood was buying the horses for himself.

However, she had no time to think about that.

She started to change into one of her attractive riding-habits.

She put the hat with its gauze veil on her head without even looking in the mirror.

Then she ran back the way she had come without waiting for anybody to guide her.

When she reached the stables it was to find that Mr. Heywood was already mounted on a very fine chestnut.

He was walking it round the cobbled yard.

There was a black stallion waiting to be saddled for the Prince and another horse beside it which Aletha knew was for her to ride.

It was a grey and was outstanding in every particular.

As she reached the Prince he said with a smile:

"I said you were a Sylph and only a Sylph could have flown so quickly."

"I am sure I have a minute to spare!" Aletha said breathlessly.

"You know I would have waited for you," he answered quietly.

She thought he would cup his hands to help her into the saddle.

Instead, he held her on each side of her small waist and lifted her.

Because he was so close, she felt a strange little tremor go through her that she did not understand.

Then he adjusted the skirt of her habit over the stirrup.

As he finished he looked up to say:

"I know I will not be disappointed when I see you ride, but if I am—I shall want to shoot myself!"

"Now you are being over-dramatic and very Hungarian!" Aletha said without thinking.

Only when his laughter rang out did she wonder if she had been rude.

*Herr* Héviz did not go with them.

The Prince led Aletha and Mr. Heywood out of the stable-yard and into some well-kept paddocks.

They passed through them.

Then Aletha found what she had always heard of— the wide, unhedged wild grassland which appeared to go into an indefinite horizon.

The horses needed no encouragement to go as fast as they wanted.

As they galloped over the grass, butterflies hovering over the flowers rose in front of them, and the song-birds swept away overhead.

To Aletha it was like riding into a Paradise she had always known existed but had never expected to find.

As she raced forward, her eyes dazzled by the sunshine, she was aware of the Prince riding beside her.

He looked very much a part of his horse.

Only when they had galloped for over a mile did they instinctively draw in their horses together.

"That was wonderful!" Aletha exclaimed. "Even more wonderful than my dreams!"

"That is what I thought when I first saw you!" the Prince replied.

She looked at him in surprise.

It was impossible to reply, for at that moment Mr. Heywood, who had been a little way behind them, drew in his horse.

"I can only say, Your Highness," he said to the Prince, "that your reputation where your horses are concerned is fully justified."

He paused a moment and then went on:

"It is impossible to find words with which to express their excellence and superiority."

"That is what I wanted you to say," the Prince replied, "but let me make clear, so there is no mistake, that the horses you are riding are not for sale!"

"I rather suspected that!" Mr. Heywood said ruefully.

"We have, however, a great many others which I know will please you," the Prince said. "Tomorrow you will ride those which can, if you wish, travel to England."

Aletha longed to say that however expensive it might be, she wanted to own the horse she was riding.

But she knew it would be a mistake to interfere.

So she said nothing and they turned for home.

As they rode back, the Prince took them by a slightly different route.

Because it was now late in the afternoon, they passed peasants returning home from their work in the fields.

They were singing as they went.

Aletha thought the girls' voices, as they mingled with the baritone of the men, were very lovely.

The Prince saw the rapt expression on her face and said:

"I knew this was what you would enjoy, and having come to Hungary you will, I know, want to hear our Gypsy music."

"Yes, of course," Aletha said. "Is it possible?"

"Nothing is impossible where you are concerned," he said, "and I will arrange for you to hear the Gypsies tomorrow night. In fact, we will have a party."

Aletha's eyes lit up, and she said:

"That is very kind of you, but we have not yet met your mother or your father."

"My mother is dead," the Prince replied, "but my father, like myself, enjoys a party, particularly if it is given for somebody very special."

Aletha wanted to say she was quite sure Prince Józsel would not think that either she or Mr. Heywood were very special.

However, she kept silent.

Later, after they had gone up to dress for dinner, Mr. Heywood came to her room to take her downstairs.

She was not alone—the maid was still there.

"I hope you are enjoying yourself," he said.

She was wearing one of the beautiful gowns that had been bought for her in London because she was to be a débutante.

It was white and the material was draped in the front over a skirt of silver lamé which clung closely to her figure.

At the back there was a bustle of white and silver ribbons.

They began as a huge bow and ended with the ends of the ribbons trailing behind her.

With every movement she made she glittered like moonlight on water.

She had known as she put it on that it would remind the Prince that he thought she was a Sylph.

She had not expected to wear any jewellery in Hungary while pretending to be Mr. Heywood's granddaughter.

But she had taken some of her mother's with her in case she needed more money.

She therefore could not resist putting a small collet of diamonds round her neck.

Then she added a brooch shaped like a star between her breasts.

Mr. Heywood was looking at her admiringly as the maid left the room.

"I suppose you realise," Aletha said in a low voice, "that we are not entitled to these bedrooms nor, I think, should we be eating in the Dining-Room."

Mr. Heywood looked puzzled.

"Prince Miklós thought you were buying horses for yourself," Aletha explained.

"Ah, now I understand," Mr. Heywood said. "I thought we were being treated differently from the way we were at first received at the Castle!"

Aletha knew that the Baron would not have offered her a diamond bracelet if he had been aware of her true identity.

Nor, she thought, would he have dared, if he had known she was her father's daughter, to enter her bedroom.

She waited for Mr. Heywood to reply, seeing that he was thinking it over before he spoke.

Then he smiled.

"Well, we may as well 'make hay while the sun shines'!" he said. "Perhaps tomorrow night we shall find ourselves moved out of the best rooms of the Palace into a pig-sty!"

"It will not be as bad as that," Aletha said, laughing, "but I shall not mind if I have to spend the night with the horse I was riding this afternoon!"

"I thought you liked that one," Mr. Heywood said, "but the Prince made it quite clear they were not for sale."

"If you ask me," Aletha said, "I think it was rather sharp practice to try and tempt us with something that was out of reach!"

Mr. Heywood laughed.

"Do not say that to His Highness or we shall definitely find ourselves sleeping in less comfortable beds!"

He walked across the room and Aletha was aware that he glanced at the lock on the door.

The key showed prominently as he opened it.

He did not say anything.

Aletha wanted to tell him she was absolutely sure there would be no need for her to lock her door that night.

The Prince had said some flattering things.

Yet her instinct told her that he would never insult her in the way the Baron had.

She did not know how she knew this, but she did know it.

She was convinced that what he felt for her was something very different.

At the same time, he was Hungarian, and she had been warned that Hungarians were romantic.

She had also read, and she was sure it was in a book she was not supposed to read, that they were very ardent and passionate lovers.

She was not certain exactly what that implied, but it was why the Baron had wanted to come to her bedroom.

It made her shudder even to think of it.

'He was not romantic,' she thought, 'just bestial, and it is degrading to think that he might have touched me!'

Prince Miklós was different.

There was something about him that reminded her of the Knights of Chivalry she had read about when she was a child.

When she thought of it, he might be like her Dream Lover.

Then she told herself she was being imaginative and quite ridiculous.

Because the Prince thought she was pretty, he had paid her compliments.

He would have complimented in the same way any woman who took his fancy.

To take him seriously would be a great mistake.

Then it suddenly struck Aletha that perhaps he was being so familiar because her grandfather was a paid servant of the Duke.

She would therefore not be a Lady, but of a lower class.

She felt as if a cold hand gripped her heart.

With an effort she made herself remember that she was in Hungary only for a few days.

Once they had bought the horses they would go home.

She would never see Prince Miklós again.

"It would be a great mistake to think too much about him," she told herself as they walked down the stairs.

The Prince was waiting for them in a very beautiful Salon, where they were to meet before dinner.

As she and Mr. Heywood entered the room, he moved from the fireplace at the end of it.

He had been talking to several other people and came towards them.

He looked so smart, so dashing, and so outstandingly handsome in his evening-clothes that Aletha felt a very strange feeling within her breast.

As he reached her she knew that for no apparent reason she was blushing.

The Prince took her hand.

"Need I tell you that you look exactly as if you had stepped from one of the fountains," he said. "And now I want to introduce you to my father."

As Aletha made a very graceful curtsy to Prince Józsel, she realised he was an older edition of his son.

His second son, Nikolas, also resembled him.

However his daughter, Misina, was attractive in a very different way.

Aletha was to learn later that she resembled her mother, who had been a Romanian Princess.

All the Estérházys were extremely pleasant to Aletha and Mr. Heywood.

The conversation at dinner was witty and so amusing, and they all seemed to be laughing.

The food was outstanding and they drank Tokay and French champagne.

They ate off Sèvres china.

Aletha thought it was infinitely preferable to the flamboyant gold plates with which the Baron had entertained them.

"What did you think of the Castle at which you stayed last night?" Prince Józsel asked Aletha.

"I was very impressed by the outside of it," she replied truthfully, "but the inside is pompous and in no way compares with Your Highness's lovely Palace."

The Prince laughed.

"That is what I thought the only time I was there."

"And what did you think of the Baron?" Prince Nikolas enquired.

The way he spoke made Aletha realise that he had already heard from his brother that she disliked the Baron.

She therefore said demurely:

"I thought he was very like his Castle!"

They all laughed, and Prince Jözsel said:

"That was a very diplomatic answer, Miss Link. It is always a mistake to make enemies, unless one is obliged to do so."

"You can say that, Papa," Misina exclaimed, "for the simple reason that people are too afraid to oppose you, and therefore you have no enemies."

"I should be more flattered," the Prince replied, "if you told me they loved me for myself."

"I think that is impossible," Misina replied, "and it applies to all of us."

"What do you mean by that?" the Prince enquired.

"Because the Estérházys have a kind of aura about us. That is what people see and think of first," his sister answered. "They are not really concerned with us as real people."

Aletha knew she had put into words exactly what she was thinking herself.

She said before anybody else could speak:

"I think if people are intelligent and sensible, they

seek what is real and true, apart from the trappings. I want to be liked just for myself and not for any other reason!"

As she spoke she saw Mr. Heywood glance at her.

She realised she had been talking as Lady Aletha Ling and not as "Miss Link."

"Of course," she added quickly, "there is no comparison between all of you here with this wonderful Palace behind you, and an ordinary person like myself."

It was rather a lame cover-up.

At the same time, she felt nobody would realise she had "made a gaffe."

Just like the French, the Estérházys loved an argument.

They were all discussing whether position, title, and wealth prevented those who had it from being human.

"Can you imagine," Misina asked scornfully, "that anybody thinks the Pope or the Emperor are just 'ordinary' men!"

"To me a woman is a woman whether she is the Empress or a peasant!" Prince Nikolas said.

He spoke very positively.

His family were aware that he was head-over-heels in love with the Empress Elizabeth.

"Frankly I think Misina is right," her father said finally. "If everybody was to be the same, the whole structure of society would collapse!"

"And a good thing too!" Prince Nikolas said.

Aletha noticed that Prince Miklós said nothing.

After dinner Misina played the piano brilliantly.

Aletha was able to listen to some of the beautiful Hungarian music, as well as melodies by Johann Strauss.

She was unaware that she swayed a little to the melody of "The Blue Danube."

Prince Miklós was watching her, and the expression in his eyes made her feel shy.

Finally when they went up to bed he escorted her to the foot of the stairs.

Mr. Heywood was having a last word with Prince Jözsel, and he said in a low voice which only she could hear:

"It makes me so happy to have you here! In your shimmering gown you not only seem part of the fountains but also of my home."

"You . . . you are flattering me," Aletha said lightly.

"I am serious," he replied, "and I shall lie awake counting the hours until tomorrow!"

Her eyes met his and she found it very difficult to look away.

Then, as she went up the stairs beside Mr. Heywood, she told herself again that she must not take him seriously.

He was just being romantic, and how could anyone be anything else when they were in Hungary?

# *chapter six*

AS Aletha dressed for dinner she thought it had been the most exciting day she had ever spent.

They had started riding the new horses which had been brought to the stables immediately after break-fast.

They were not as impressive as those which the Prince wished to keep.

At the same time, a lot of them were young and had tremendous possibilities.

Aletha knew from the look on Mr. Heywood's face that he was more than delighted with what the Prince had produced.

It seemed inevitable, Aletha thought, that she should ride beside the Prince.

Mr. Heywood went off on his own, taking jumps unexpectedly so as to test the horse he was on.

Occasionally he would gallop off, only to return looking more pleased than he had before he started.

"It is hopeless," Aletha said to Prince Miklós during the afternoon. "My grandfather obviously finds it impossible to choose which are the best."

The Prince laughed.

"I assure you we are only too willing to sell those we do not want for ourselves."

"That is the whole point," Aletha replied. "You are being greedy!"

"I am also greedy about other things besides horses."

He was looking at her as he spoke with the expression in his eyes she had begun to expect.

Every time she was aware of it she felt a little tremor in her breast.

She knew that being with him was not only interesting, but also thrilling.

'When I go home,' she thought, 'I shall never see him again, so it is no use feeling like this!'

But she could not suppress what she was feeling, nor could she stop herself from knowing that her heart turned over when he paid her a compliment.

"You are too good to be true!" he said. "Ever since I met you I find it hard to believe you are real."

"My father once said that if you prick a King, he bleeds, and that makes sure he is a human being."

She expected the Prince to give her some witty answer.

Instead, he looked away from her.

When she glanced at him in surprise she knew instinctively that he wished to say that he wanted to kiss her.

The idea did not shock her, nor did she feel disgusted, as she had when the Baron had spoken of her lips.

'Perhaps it would be very exciting to be kissed by a Hungarian in Hungary,' she thought, 'and certainly very romantic!'

Then, as she glanced at the Prince, she knew he was reading her thoughts.

For a moment they just looked at each other.

"I suppose you know," he said, "you are torturing me unbearably! The sooner you go back to England the better!"

He spoke so violently that she stared at him in astonishment.

Without speaking another word he turned his horse and started to gallop back towards the Palace.

After a few seconds she started to follow him.

He rode ahead until they reached the entrance to the stables.

Then he waited.

She rode up beside him and he said:

"Forgive me! Sometimes you torture me beyond endurance!"

She looked at him in bewilderment.

As if he realised she had no idea what he was talking about, he said gently:

"Forget me! I want you to enjoy yourself, and I suspect your grandfather will soon make up his mind. Then you will be leaving Hungary behind."

"But I will have . . . your horses to remind me of . . . your wonderful . . . country," Aletha replied.

She wanted to say: "to remind me of you."

But she knew that was something which was far too intimate.

As if once again he knew what she was thinking, he put out his hand.

After a moment's pause she gave him hers.

She had pulled off her glove.

As their bare skin touched, she felt something like a streak of lightning run through her.

Then, as the Prince took off his hat and bent to kiss her hand, she knew that she loved him.

It was something she had never meant to do, something she had never expected.

Yet, as her love surged through her, she knew this was what she had always longed to feel for the man of her dreams.

Of course that was what he was!

She wondered how she could not have been aware of it when he had spoken to her on the Terrace of the Royal Palace.

'I love . . . you! I . . . love you!' she wanted to say.

As she felt the hard pressure of his lips on the softness of her skin her fingers trembled.

He was aware of it, and he raised his head to look at her.

To her surprise, there was not the glow of admiration in his eyes but an unaccountable look of pain.

It was something she did not understand.

The Prince released her hand, put his hat back on his head, and rode ahead of her into the stables.

She followed him, feeling bewildered.

Mr. Heywood was talking to *Herr* Héviz.

Aletha knew they were discussing the price of a dozen horses that were being led round them by a groom.

She slipped from her horse's back without any assistance and walked away from the stables towards the Palace.

She hoped, because she could not help herself, that Prince Miklós would follow her.

But she knew that when he dismounted he had joined Mr. Heywood.

As she went up to her bedroom to change, she tried to puzzle out why he had behaved in such a strange manner.

She thought she knew the answer but did not want to admit it to herself.

In fact, her whole being shied away from what she suspected was the truth.

As if to soothe her feelings, she told herself that of course the dashing and romantic Hungarians were unpredictable.

How could they be anything else?

She did not change and go downstairs.

She thought that doubtless the ladies of the party would be congregated in one of the beautiful Drawing-Rooms.

She felt she could not bear to make light conversation.

Every nerve in her body was pulsating towards the Prince.

She therefore took off her habit, undressed, and got into bed.

"I will call you in plenty of time for your bath, *Fräulein*," the maid promised.

She dropped her a curtsy before she left the room.

Aletha knew that if she were staying there as her father's daughter, it would have been a much deeper one.

The House-keeper would also have curtsied instead of just inclining her head.

She did not particularly wish for such obsequi-
ousness.

At the same time, it told her what she already
knew.

There was a great difference between being a
Duke's daughter and the grandchild of a man who
could not afford to buy his own horses.

She had only to meet the Prince's father and the
other members of his family to know how excessively
proud they were.

Aletha had to admit that in a way her father was
the same.

Yet perhaps it was not so obvious in England as it
was in Hungary.

As they had ridden past the peasants coming back
from the fields, all the women had curtsied to the
Prince.

The men had swept their hats from their heads and
bowed deeply.

They had also smiled at him with affection.

It was an affection tinged with respect that made
him seem almost god-like.

'I suppose it is very childish of me to love him,'
Aletha thought as she took her bath. 'I expect really
I am just infatuated with his glamour and the Fairy
Tale background of the Palace.'

She thought it was exactly the right setting for the
Prince of her Dreams, if that was what he was.

She had learned there were 126 rooms in the Palace.

Prince Jözsel was continually speaking of how much
more magnificent it had been when first erected by his
ancestor.

The Opera House had been burned down and never rebuilt.

Aletha tried to laugh at herself for being as impressed as the Prince expected her to be.

'I could tell him that Ling, in its own way, is just as grand,' she thought, 'and actually the building itself is older!'

Then she laughed at herself again for being so childish.

She got out of her bath.

The maid helped her to dress in what she thought was the prettiest gown she had brought with her.

It was white and embroidered all over with tiny diamanté.

It made her look as if she were a flower sparkled with tiny drops of dew.

The impression was accentuated by the white flowers with diamanté on their petals which ornamented her neck.

Diamanté also glittered on the small bustle at the back where there were flowers caught in the folds of chiffon.

Tonight Aletha wore no jewellery.

The same flowers, which were something like white orchids, were arranged at the back of her head.

When she went into the Salon before dinner she thought Prince Miklós drew in his breath.

A number of other men who had been invited to dinner stared at her with undisguised admiration.

"Now I know why the Estérházy Palace looks more beautiful than it ever has in the past!" one of them said to her.

She smiled at the compliment and felt her heart

give a leap as she realised that the Prince was looking angry.

She knew he was jealous.

She thought how wonderful it would be if he should love her as she loved him.

Then she told herself it was too much to ask.

How could she expect that she would fall in love with the first really handsome man she had ever met?

How could she expect him to feel the same about her?

"Hungarians are romantic!" she kept repeating to herself. "Romantic!"

That meant, she knew, they would make love to every pretty woman they met, but she would not mean anything in their life.

Of course they would flit from flower to flower!

They would always be hoping they would find a more beautiful one the next day than they had found the day before.

"I have to be sensible about this," she murmured.

Yet she enjoyed every moment of the dinner.

She found that nearly every man at the table was raising his glass to her in a toast.

The other young women were looking at her sour-ly.

She had already learnt that in London débutantes were not of any great importance, except for one moment when they were presented at Buckingham Palace.

They attended the Balls to which they were invited because their fathers were distinguished men.

But they were over-shadowed by the sophisticated

married Beauties who were acclaimed not only by Society, but by the public, and singled out by the Prince of Wales.

"This is my glorious hour," Aletha told herself, "so I had better make the most of it."

As the Prince had promised, she found they were to have a Gypsy Orchestra in the huge, magnificent white and gold Ball-Room.

It was here Haydn had conducted the first performance of his "Farewell Symphony."

It was the most beautiful Ball-Room Aletha had ever imagined.

The flowers that decorated it were all white, which complemented her gown.

The tall windows were open to the splendid gardens outside.

Lights were hidden in the fountains which illuminated the water they flung towards the diamond-studded sky.

The Gypsy Orchestra was exactly what she had expected it would be.

The Gypsy women were dressed in their brilliantly-coloured costumes.

The women wore huge ear-rings and a profusion of bracelets on their arms.

Their headdresses of red ribbons were ornamented with gold and precious stones.

They sparkled and glittered with every movement they made.

The music started with the clash of cymbals, the bell-like ring of tambourines.

Then the volume lifted the wild, joyous music of a Gypsy dance up to the sky.

Amongst the guests, some of the young girls and men moved hand-in-hand in a traditional Gypsy dance in the centre of the room.

Then the music changed and became sweeter and more tender.

The Prince put his arm around Aletha and drew her onto the floor.

Everybody began to dance, and the music became compelling and romantic.

After a little time the wildness came back into the Gypsy instruments.

Those who were dancing moved quicker and quicker.

Aletha had found herself dancing with various other men, but now once again she was with the Prince.

He drew her closer to him.

To her surprise, she found she could follow his steps exactly, even though she had never learnt them.

Quicker and quicker the rhythm rose, and quicker and quicker they moved.

Then, as the dance grew even wilder, she felt as if he carried her into the air.

Their feet were not moving on the ground; rather, they flew like birds.

It was exciting and exhilarating and, when finally the music stopped, Aletha was breathless.

She also felt as if she were tumbling down from a great height back to reality.

Prince Miklós still had his arm around her.

As she looked up at him her breasts were moving tempestuously beneath the soft chiffon of her gown.

She thought there was a fire in his eyes, but told herself it was only a reflection of the light.

The guests were applauding the music which had carried them away.

Aletha thought they danced with their hearts and not their feet.

The Prince was drawing her from the Ball-Room into the garden.

She took a deep breath of the night air, as if somehow it could soothe the tumult within her.

The Prince put her arm through his, and they walked past the fountains and over the soft green lawn.

They reached some bushes covered in blossom.

They passed through them and surprisingly there was a glass-house shining amongst the trees.

The Prince opened the door.

As they entered, Aletha saw that the whole place was filled with orchids.

They were white, purple, green, pink, and every other colour.

In some unusual manner they were lit from the floor.

They were so lovely that Aletha stood looking at them as if spellbound.

The Prince shut the door.

Then he said:

"This is the right place for you! I thought perhaps you could dissolve into the flowers you resemble. Then I would never lose you!"

Slowly, because she was a little shy, Aletha turned her head to look at him.

She thought as she did so that no man could look more handsome or so magnificent.

His evening-clothes fitted tightly to his slim, athletic body.

He wore one large pearl in the centre of his white shirt.

Aletha knew that if it were a more formal occasion and Royalty had been present, his coat would have been covered with decorations.

Her eyes met his, and they just stood looking at each other.

At last he said:

"You are so incredibly lovely, so beautiful, that you will always be in my heart!"

Aletha was about to reply that he would always be in hers when he added:

"I have brought you here tonight to say goodbye to you."

"Goodbye?" Aletha repeated. "I . . . I did not . . . know that we were . . . leaving . . . tomorrow!"

"It is not you who are leaving," the Prince replied, "it is I!"

Aletha could only look at him wide-eyed.

Then he said harshly:

"I am crucifying myself and I cannot stand being tortured any longer!"

"I . . . I do not . . . understand!" Aletha stammered.

"I know that," the Prince replied. "I know every thought in your exquisite head, every breath you breathe, every beat of your heart!"

The way he spoke made Aletha quiver with the feelings he aroused in her.

Instinctively she put her hand to her breast to quell the tumult within it.

"I love you!" the Prince said. "I love you as I have never loved a woman before. That is why, Heart of my Heart, I have to go away."

"But . . . why . . . why?" Aletha asked. "I do not . . . understand!"

"Of course not," he said. "You are so unspoilt, so utterly desirable. I want to take you in my arms and carry you with me to my house in the mountains, where we would be alone with no one to disturb us."

Aletha felt her whole body tremble with a strange excitement.

There was a fire in the Prince's eyes she had never seen before.

"Once we were there, my lovely one," he said, "I would teach you about love—not the cold love that an Englishman would give you, but the wild, burning, irresistible love of Hungary!"

Because the way he spoke was so compelling, Aletha instinctively took a step towards him.

To her surprise, he moved away from her.

"Do not come near me!" he said harshly. "I dare not touch you! If I do, I will make you mine! Then you could never escape and I would never let you go again."

"You . . . you love . . . me?" Aletha stammered as if it were the only thing she understood in all he was saying.

"I love you!" the Prince said. "I love you wildly, uncontrollably, irrevocably. But, my sweet, my precious, there is nothing I can do about it."

"W-why? Why . . . not?"

"The answer, quite simply, is that you are like these flowers, pure and unspoilt. How could I damage anything so beautiful, so perfect?"

Aletha continued to stare at him.

Then, as the starlight touched her hair, he turned away as if he could not bear to look at her.

"I do not think I ought to put it into words," he said, "but it would be unfair to leave you wondering."

"Please . . . tell me . . . please explain . . . what you are . . . saying," Aletha said piteously.

"I have told you I love you," the Prince said, "and I believe you love me a little."

Aletha made a little murmur and he went on:

"I can imagine nothing nearer to Heaven than to take your love and make it a part of mine, which it is already."

He made a sound which was one of pain as he added:

"But it is something I dare not do."

"Why not . . . please . . . tell me . . . why not."

"Because, my precious, beautiful little English girl, you are a lady. If you were not, if you were just the relative of an ordinary man who bought and sold horses like Héviz, I would take you away with me, and I think, my beloved, we would be very happy together."

Aletha did not make a sound.

She was beginning to understand what he was saying, and she felt as if her whole body were turning to stone.

The Prince made a gesture with his hand.

"That way is barred, and because of my family, I cannot make you my wife."

The words had been said, and to Aletha they seemed to ring out.

She wondered why the orchids did not fall to the

floor and the glass that covered them smash and scatter into pieces.

"You have seen my father," the Prince was saying, "and you are imaginative enough to know that it would break his heart if, as the eldest son, I took as my wife anyone who was not the equal of our blood."

Aletha did not move.

She only felt very cold, as if the blood had drained away from her body and her life had gone with it.

"From the first moment I saw you," the Prince said, "I knew you were something special, something different from anyone I had met before. As you stood at the balustrade outside the Royal Palace, it was as if you were surrounded with a white light, and I thought no one could be more lovely!"

The Prince put his hands over his eyes for a moment as he said:

"I could not sleep for thinking about you. The following days and nights you were always with me until I believed I was haunted."

He paused for a moment before he said, and his voice was raw:

"Then you came back, and for one moment I was wildly, ecstatically happy, just because you were there."

His voice deepened as he said:

"Nothing else seemed to matter. I merely waited for the moment when I could hold you in my arms and kiss you until we could no longer think of anything but each other."

Aletha knew that was what she wanted too.

Yet she could not speak as the Prince continued:

"There is no need for me to say that you ride better than any woman I have ever known. You even equal the Empress herself—but that is immaterial."

He stared at her before he said:

"It is not what you do, what you say, or even what you think. It is something Divine within yourself which I searched for, dreamt of, but thought I would never find."

Aletha knew that was what she felt about him.

She wanted to cry out and beg him not to destroy anything so perfect as their love.

But the words would not come to her lips and he continued:

"If I made you my wife, which I want more than my own salvation, it would be impossible for me to make you happy because though we would be in Heaven while we were together, we would have to live in the world as it is."

He drew in his breath before he went on:

"My family would never forgive me for making what to them would be a *mésalliance*. It would hurt you not once, but a thousand times a day to know what they were saying, what they would do, and what they would think."

He paused a moment and then went on:

"It would be impossible for me to protect you, and gradually, like water dripping onto a stone, it would destroy our love."

He drew himself up and seemed to grow taller as he said:

"That is why, my darling, I am going away tomorrow, and after that we shall never see each other again."

There was a despair in his voice that made Aletha want to reach out her arms towards him.

She wanted to tell him that he need not suffer, that she could sweep away his unhappiness.

As she was trying to find the right words he said:

"Goodbye, my lovely Sylph. I pray God will protect you and that one day you will find a man who will love you as I do, and who would take his own life rather than hurt you in any way."

He looked at her for a moment.

Then he went down on one knee, and raising the hem of her gown, kissed it.

Aletha looked at him in astonishment.

As he rose she said in a voice that hardly sounded like her own:

"Miklós . . . wait . . . I have something to . . . tell you . . . !"

Even as she spoke he was gone.

He had opened the door of the glass-house and disappeared into the shadows outside before the sentence was finished.

Aletha stared after him.

It was then she put up her hands to cover her eyes.

Could this really have happened?

Could she really have heard Prince Miklós tell her that he loved her?

At the same time, he would not marry her.

'I must . . . tell him,' she thought. 'I must . . . tell him he is . . . mistaken and that his . . . family would . . . accept me . . . and we can be together . . . and we can be . . . happy.'

She took a step towards the open door.

Suddenly a pride she had not known she possessed made her stand still again.

If he was so intuitive, if he really, as he said, could read her thoughts, her feelings, and understand the beating of her heart, why did he not know the truth?

Why was he not aware that her blood was as blue as his own?

Why did he not guess that her family were as important in England as the Estérházys were in Hungary?

He should have known, he should have known intuitively that she was not what she pretended to be.

How long she stood surrounded by the orchids with the stars shining through the glass above her head, Aletha had no idea.

When at last she realised she must go back to the Palace, she moved slowly, as if in a dream.

It was then she told herself that her dream had ended.

The Man of her Dreams had failed her.

"If he were really so closely attuned to me, he would have known that I am I, and my Family Tree is not of the least consequence."

She reached a side door of the Palace and slipped upstairs.

The Gypsy Orchestra was still playing in the Ball-Room.

There was still the sound of voices and laughter.

Aletha went to her bedroom.

She did not ring for the maid who she knew would be waiting to help her.

Instead, slowly, with stiff fingers that did not seem like her own, she took off the beautiful white gown.

The dew-drops were still glistening on the flowers.

She removed the flowers from her hair and let it fall over her shoulders.

It seemed to take her a long time to undress and get into bed.

Only when she had blown out the candle and was in darkness did she hide her face in her pillow.

It was then the tears began to fall.

They were tears of despair, not only because she had lost Miklós and her heart.

He had also destroyed her dream.

## *chapter seven*

ALETHA cried despondently until she was exhausted.

Then she lay awake thinking that her Castle of Dreams had fallen in ruins about her.

Never again would she dream of a man who would love her for herself.

It was exactly the reverse of what she had expected to happen.

In England her father had been convinced she would be married because she was the daughter of a Duke.

In Hungary the Prince thought she was not good enough for his family, and his love was not strong enough to fight them single-handed.

Like a child who has been hurt, she wanted to go home.

She wanted to leave Hungary now, at this very moment.

She wanted to find herself at Ling with all that was familiar about her.

Hungary had given her feelings she had never expected.

She knew it was the passion that comes with love and is part of love.

When it touched the soul it was Divine.

'I must leave,' she thought, 'whatever Mr. Heywood says.'

He was quick-brained, and he would doubtless by now have decided which of the horses he wanted.

It would merely be a question of price and arranging for them to be safely transported to England.

"I will tell him that we must leave as soon as he is awake," she told herself.

It was still dark outside, but the stars were fading.

She pulled back the curtains.

Then she stood at the window, waiting for the first fingers of the dawn to appear on the horizon.

When they did, she knew it was still too early to approach Mr. Heywood.

"I will go riding," she decided.

She would ride in Hungary for the last time.

After that she would try to forget the wild gallops before the wild emotions that the Prince had aroused in her.

She told herself despairingly that she would never feel them again.

Her marriage would be conventional.

Because she no longer cared, she would accept the husband her father chose for her.

It was bitter to know that she only had to tell Prince Miklós who she really was, and everything would be changed.

But however persuasive he might be, she knew she would never trust his love, never believe it was what he felt for her.

"If he had been one of the peasants we saw yesterday coming back from the fields," she told herself, "I would marry him and be happy in a cottage, loving him and our children."

This again was all part of her imagination, as unreal as the romance of Hungary and, in a way, the Palace itself.

It was too beautiful, too perfect, too dream-like to be substantial enough on which to build a future without true love, the love which, as the Prince had said, was irresistible.

But it was not irresistible enough for him to sacrifice his pride, and the pride in his family.

"I must . . . leave," she cried, and started to dress.

She felt she could not be confined at the moment within the walls of the Palace.

The Prince was too near her.

Perhaps by the time she returned from her ride he would have left as he had said he intended to do.

Then she would never see him again and she prayed that she would forget him.

She put on a thin blouse and her riding-skirt.

Then she picked up her jacket and hesitated.

Yesterday had been hot and she had the idea that today would be hotter still, in which case, if she intended to ride hard and fast, she would not need more than her blouse to cover her.

There would be nobody to see her.

She pinned her hair tightly at the back of her head, and did not wear a hat.

When she was ready she left her room very quietly so that no one would hear.

She moved along the corridor to where there was a secondary staircase.

She knew there would be a footman on duty in the hall.

As she went she glanced in a mirror and thought her face was very pale.

Her eyes seemed enormous and she knew the darkness in them was due to the pain she was suffering.

It made her feel as if there were a hundred arrows piercing her heart.

She found her way without any difficulty to the door through which the Prince had taken her the first day she arrived to the stables.

By the time she reached them the sun was shining and turning everything to gold.

It was far too early for *Herr* Héviz to be about.

She found a stable-boy who had been on duty during the night.

She told him she wanted to ride Nyul, the grey she had ridden the first afternoon.

By the time Nyul was saddled, another groom had appeared and asked if he should accompany her.

She understood enough Hungarian to tell him she was going only a little way and wished to be on her own.

She thought he looked surprised, but he was young and did not expostulate as *Herr* Héviz would have.

She rode out of the stables on the superb grey.

She forced herself to think of nothing except the horse she was riding.

"Now I can forget everything except you," she told Nyul.

She rode through the paddocks and out through the

way they had been before to reach the meadowland.

The rising sun had already brought out the butterflies, and they were fluttering over the flowers.

Just as they had done before, they rose in front of her like an elusive cloud.

The birds, disturbed by her approach, soared up into the sky.

Nyul was fresh, and Aletha gave him his head.

He sprang forward and she was riding as swiftly as the flight of a bird.

On and on they went until Aletha felt as if the hard lump of misery within her breast softened a little.

Now the sunshine was dazzling her eyes.

She thought that the beauty all around her was some consolation for the darkness within her heart.

She rode on farther and farther, deep in her thoughts.

Suddenly in the distance she saw coming towards her two men on horseback.

She thought it an intrusion that they should be encroaching on her.

For the moment she was in a world in which she was completely alone.

She was just about to turn round and go back the way she had come.

Then she realised there was something familiar about the two riders.

As she stared in their direction she knew with a sensation of shock that one was the Baron.

He was riding a very large stallion which she remembered as being the best in his stables.

The groom beside him also rode a horse that was larger than the average.

There was no doubt it was the man she had no wish ever to see again.

Then she was aware that the Baron had recognised her.

The two horsemen were still some distance away, but she saw him bringing down his whip sharply on the stallion.

He spoke to his groom, who also swept forward, at the same time moving out from beside him.

It was then Aletha's intuition that told her she was in danger.

Almost as if she heard the order the Baron gave, she knew he intended to come up on one side of her and the groom on the other.

Then she would be helpless and at their mercy.

Without wasting any more time, she turned Nyul's head for home.

As she did so, she realised she had come much farther than she had intended.

The Palace was not in sight, and she was no longer at the point where the Prince had turned to take them back by a different route.

She galloped for some distance, then looked back.

The Baron was far nearer to her than he had been before.

He was bending over his horse and riding almost jockey-style to overtake.

She was aware then that her sense of danger was not mistaken.

She shuddered to think what might happen if she became a captive of the Baron.

It might be a long time before Mr. Heywood or

anyone in the Palace had any idea to where she had been taken.

"Help me . . . oh, God . . . help me!" she prayed as she heard the Baron's horse thundering along behind her.

Nyul was certainly doing his best.

At the same time, they had already ridden a long way at full gallop before Aletha had become aware of the Baron.

Now Aletha was riding faster than she had ever done in her whole life.

Yet she knew the Baron was gaining on her.

She thought as she tried to go faster still that she would rather die than be in his power.

\*　　\*　　\*

Prince Miklós had also spent a sleepless night.

When he had left Aletha among the orchids in the glass-house he had walked blindly across the garden.

He wanted to get away from the music and the sound of laughter.

He knew that what he was doing would break his heart and haunt him for ever.

But he had been brought up to know how great his heritage was.

It had been drummed into him that he must dedicate his whole life to being as fine and brave as his ancestors had been.

His father had said to him when he was a small boy that whatever sacrifices he had to make he must accept them willingly.

He must not fail those who had preceded him and those who would follow.

Miklós had not quite understood at the time.

He had, however, learnt as he grew older that his duty to his family was more important than his own desires.

At School he had worked not for himself.

By being as clever and intelligent as his father, he would not fail the family when it was his turn to be the reigning Prince.

Of course there had been women in his life.

From the moment he was old enough they pursued him, tried to seduce him and make themselves indispensable.

They captured his body and he found them fascinating.

But some critical part of his brain told him they were not good enough for the position he had to offer.

His mother had been of Royal Blood and had loved her husband and her family more than anything in the world.

For Miklós she was the standard by which he judged every woman who was offered to him as a wife.

He always found them lacking.

He knew now that he would never love anyone as he loved Aletha.

From the first moment they had met he had known they were already part of each other.

As he had told her, he had seen her enveloped with a Divine light.

When she came to the Palace, he could read her thoughts and sense her feelings.

He knew that she was the woman who had been meant for him by God.

Even the Sacrament of Matrimony would not bind them any closer than they were already.

But his brain told him that marriage with a woman whose grandfather was a paid servant of the Duke of Buclington was impossible.

The ancestor after whom he was named had built the Palace.

Ever since then the Estérházys had encouraged the greatest Musicians, Artists, and the finest brains of the country to come to Fertōd.

They had all served the family in one way or another.

"Served" was the operative word.

Franz Joseph Haydn might have been the greatest Musician of his age, but there could have been no question of his marrying an Estérházy.

The same applied to the Artists, the Architects, the Poets, and the Writers.

All of them were welcome, but only to "serve" the family in their various ways, certainly not become a part of it.

Perhaps the women who bore the name of Estérházy were even more proud and more implacable than the men.

Prince Miklós knew there was not one of them, including his sister, Misina, who would accept Aletha as her equal.

How could he find tranquility or happiness in the Palace in those circumstances?

He had to live there: it was part of his Kingdom.

He had to minister to those who bore his name, in the same way as his ancestors had done.

They had built up a Kingdom within a Kingdom.

They all, Miklós thought, bowed to the Emperor, but privately they considered themselves superior to an Austrian.

When finally Prince Miklós walked back to the Palace, the music was silent and the guests had departed.

The lights had been extinguished in most of the windows.

He went to his bedroom to pull back the curtains from the windows.

He felt he must have more air to go on breathing.

He did not undress, but just pulled off his evening-coat.

Then he sat with his head in his hands and suffered as he had never suffered before in the whole of his life.

When dawn came he knew he had to get away so that there would be no chance of seeing Aletha again.

Even to think of seeing her made the blood throb in his temples.

Every instinct in his body told him to carry her away to his house in the mountains and make her his.

They would be happy—deliriously, wonderfully, blissfully happy.

But there was always tomorrow.

Tomorrow and the years that came after it, years when eventually he would have to leave her and she would never forgive him.

He rang the bell for his Valet, and when the man came, told him to pack.

Because he had no wish to see anyone and have

to make explanations or answer questions, he ordered breakfast in his room.

Having bathed and changed his clothes, he stood at the window.

He looked out blindly over the flower-filled garden.

Beyond was the meadowland where he had galloped with Aletha.

It was separated from the gardens by a brick wall that surrounded the whole Palace.

Then he was aware there were three horses in the far distance.

At that range they were little larger than dots.

They seemed to be moving towards the Palace.

He watched them only vaguely, immersed in his own unhappiness.

Suddenly he saw, although he could hardly believe his eyes, that the leading horse was Nyul and Aletha was riding him.

He watched her as she rode, leaning forward, straining every nerve to make the grey go faster.

Because he thought it strange, he looked past her.

She was being followed by two men.

With a sense of shock he realised that one of them was Baron Otto von Sicardsburg.

He definitely recognised him, also the big black stallion of which he was told the Baron continually boasted.

It was then he knew almost as if she had called out to him that Aletha was frightened.

He knew her fear was for what the Baron obviously intended.

He wanted to curse him.

At the same time, he wanted to assure Aletha that whatever happened, he would save and protect her.

There was no doubt now that the Baron was gaining and was in fact only a few lengths behind her.

In front of them there was no opening into the Palace garden, only the brick wall.

Then, as Miklós realised what Aletha meant to do, he felt as if he were facing a firing-squad.

\* \* \*

Aletha was conscious of the fact that the Baron was close behind her.

She had reached the Palace but did not turn in the direction that would lead her towards the stables.

To do so meant that she would have to pull Nyul in and the Baron would certainly overtake her.

She was sure he intended to snatch at her reins.

She would be powerless to stop herself from being led away beside the black stallion, back to the Baron's Castle.

"Save . . . me! Save . . . me!" she cried in her heart.

Then as the brick wall loomed ahead she knew what she must do.

She had never jumped on Nyul.

Anyway, the wall was too high and too solid to risk anything so dangerous.

But it was her only hope.

She spoke to Nyul, feeling he would understand.

As she gathered him for the jump, he leapt into the air, carrying her into the sky almost as if he had wings.

It would have been impossible, she knew, for any

ordinary horse to manage such a jump.

Incredibly, Aletha was to think afterwards, it must have been with the help of God and His Angels that Nyul cleared it with just an inch to spare.

The horse landed, again by good fortune, in a flower-bed.

He staggered, nearly fell, but then regained his balance.

He was sweating and for the moment completely exhausted.

Aletha kept her seat but was almost unconscious with the effort.

She shut her eyes and her head dropped on her breast.

Her hair had come loose with the speed at which she had ridden.

It fell over her shoulders in a gold cloud.

She had released the reins and was holding on to the saddle.

She felt the whole world slipping away from her.

Then strong arms were lifting her down from the saddle.

A voice which seemed to come from far away was saying:

"My darling! My sweet! How could you have done anything so dangerous? I thought you were going to kill yourself!"

She could not answer, but could only lie limp in Prince Miklós's arms.

Her head was resting on his shoulder.

He went down on one knee to hold her close against him.

The strength of his arms told her she was safe.

As he looked down at her pale face, her closed eyes

and her hair, something broke within him.

Wildly, passionately, he kissed her forehead, her eyes, her cheeks, and her lips.

He drew her back to life, and it was the only way he could express his joy that she was not dead.

To Aletha it was as if she had stepped from a Hell of fear into a Heaven of happiness.

It was impossible to open her eyes.

She still felt as if she had drifted a long way into oblivion.

At the same time, she could feel his kisses.

As he held her lips captive, something flickered within her heart and she knew it was life itself.

"I love you! I love you!" Miklós was saying. "And I thought I had lost you!"

Because there was a note of agony in his voice, Aletha opened her eyes.

His face was very near to hers.

When she saw his expression she knew how frightened he had been that she would be killed.

"I . . . I am . . . alive," she wanted to say.

But her lips could not part before he was kissing her again.

Then very gently he stood up and drew her to her feet.

"I am going to carry you into the house," he said.

As if he could not help himself, he kissed her again.

Now her whole being responded and she thought that lightning flashed in her breast.

There were little flames riding up her throat and touching her lips.

Miklós's voice was deep and very moving as he said:

"You are mine! Mine completely, and I know now I cannot live without you! How soon will you marry me, my darling?"

She stared at him.

"Are you . . . really asking me . . . to . . . marry you?" she whispered.

They were the first words she had spoken since Nyul had jumped over the wall.

"You will marry me," Miklós answered, "if I have to fight the whole world to make you my wife!"

It was so wonderful to hear the words she had longed to hear him say that Alctha shut her eyes again.

He picked her up in his arms and started to carry her towards the Palace.

Only when they had gone a little way did Aletha say in a voice he could hardly hear:

"Do you . . . really love me . . . enough to . . . make me your . . . w-wife?"

"No one and nothing is of any importance except you!" Miklós replied.

His lips touched her forehead before he went on:

"It will not be easy, but I love and worship you, and we will pray that nothing else will ever be of any consequence."

"Nothing . . . will . . . be," Aletha murmured.

They reached a side door of the Palace and Miklós took her inside.

Aletha was suddenly conscious of her hair falling about her shoulders.

"I . . . I do not . . . want to be . . . seen," she whispered.

Miklós smiled.

He put her down but kept his arm around her.

He opened the door of a room that was not far from where they had come in.

It was one of the many small but beautiful Sitting-Rooms on the Ground Floor of the Palace.

All the pictures were by French Artists such as Bucher, Fragonard, and Greuze.

The furniture was also French.

"This is a room for love," he said as he shut the door, "and I am going to tell you, my darling, how much I love you!"

He picked her up again in his arms.

Sitting down on the sofa, he cradled her against him as if she were a child.

Then he was kissing her passionately, demandingly, and possessively.

Once again they were flying in the sky, and it was impossible to believe there was the world beneath them.

\* \* \*

It was a long time later and, although they had not spoken, Aletha felt as if they had said a thousand things to each other.

There was no need for explanations, no need for anything but love.

"How can you make me feel like this?" Miklós exclaimed.

"Like . . . what?" Aletha asked for the sheer joy of hearing him say it.

"It is something I have never felt before. But then, I have never loved anyone as I love you!"

"Could . . . anything be more . . . wonderful?" Aletha said. "And I . . . was so . . . unhappy last . . . night."

"You are not to think about it anymore," Miklós ordered. "I was mad, crazy, to think that we could ever be without each other!"

The fire was once again back in his eyes as he said:

"You are mine, and I will kill any other man who tries to touch you!"

"I . . . I think the . . . Baron intended to take me prisoner," Aletha said.

"To escape him you might have killed yourself!"

There was a note of horror in Miklós's voice that was very moving.

"But . . . I am alive . . . and . . . I am here."

"You are, my precious, and now we are going to be married immediately!"

He put her down as he spoke and rose to his feet.

"I do not intend to waste any more time," he said. "We will go and tell my father that you are to be my wife and there is nothing he or anyone else can say or do to prevent us from being married at once!"

Aletha stared at him in surprise.

Then, as he was kissing her again, it was impossible to tell him the words that trembled on her lips.

As he set her free, she had a sudden glimpse of herself in a gold-framed mirror.

She was horrified at the untidiness of her appearance.

"Let me first go and change," she said quickly, "and then I have something to tell you."

Miklós glanced at the clock.

"They will have finished breakfast," he said, "and my father will be alone, dealing with his correspondence."

He stopped to look at her lovingly before he went on:

"But hurry, otherwise he may become involved with other members of the family before we can tell him what we are planning to do."

Aletha had no wish for anyone to see her as she looked at this moment.

She therefore allowed Miklós to take her up a side staircase.

He left her at her bedroom door.

"I will come back for you, my Lovely One, in ten minutes," he said, "so hurry! I am afraid of being away from you even for a minute!"

"I will . . . still be . . . here," Aletha promised with a smile.

She knew he wanted to kiss her again, and she quickly went into her bedroom.

She rang for the maid.

By the time she arrived, Aletha had already washed and taken off her riding-skirt and blouse.

She put on one of her prettiest gowns and had just finished arranging her hair when there was a knock on the door.

She knew it was Miklós.

She could not help running across the room.

It was with the greatest difficulty that she did not throw herself into his arms.

"I am . . . ready!" she said breathlessly.

"You look very lovely!" he answered. "I am determined that we shall be married tonight, or at the very latest tomorrow!"

She wanted to tell him why it was impossible.

Then she saw a servant coming down the passage.

She was silent as Miklós took her down the stairs.

They went across the hall and down another corridor which led them to his father's Study.

Aletha knew it was a very impressive room.

She thought if she did not have a secret which would surprise them all she would have been nervous.

Instead, with her hand in Miklós's, she felt as if her heart and the whole world were singing.

He loved her!

He loved her enough to marry her, whoever she might be.

He opened the door of the Study.

As they went in, Aletha felt a stab of disappointment as she saw that the Prince was not alone.

Standing beside him at the window was another man.

Then, as the two men turned round, Aletha gave a gasp.

It was her father who stood there.

He looked tall and very distinguished.

"Papa!"

Her voice rang out as she ran towards him.

She flung herself against him.

"You are . . . here! How is it . . . possible? Why have . . . you come?"

The words seemed to fall over themselves as her father put his arms round her.

Then he said:

"The King of Denmark was ill and therefore all the festivities were cancelled. So I returned home to find my daughter had been very naughty and had run away!"

Aletha drew in her breath.

"Were you . . . very . . . angry?" she asked in a small voice.

"Very," the Duke replied, "if I had not been aware that John Heywood would take good care of you. But I did not expect to find that in buying my horses for me, he had also taken on the role of your grandfather!"

His eyes were twinkling as he spoke and Aletha knew he was not really angry with her.

It was then she looked at Miklós and saw his astonishment.

She put out her hand towards him.

"This was the . . . secret I . . . wanted to . . . tell you," she said.

She thought for a moment that perhaps he would be angry because she had deceived him.

Then he answered.

"Can it really be true that you are the daughter of the Duke?"

"It is really true," the Duke said before Aletha could reply, "and I have been apologising to the Prince because my daughter has been deceiving you all!"

"Of course I understand," Prince Józsel said, "that in the circumstances, it was the only way that Lady Aletha could travel if she had no proper chaperone."

"Well, I will look after her now," the Duke said.

He spoke as if he thought he must gloss over anything that might affect Aletha's reputation.

"At least, Your Highness, I shall now have the pleasure of seeing your horses for myself."

"And, of course, riding them," Prince Józsel added.

Aletha drew herself from her father's arms.

"Now that you are here, Papa," she said, "there is something more important than even the horses, and Miklós will tell you what it is."

The Duke held out his hand to Prince Miklós.

"I guessed that was who you were," he said, "and I am delighted to have the pleasure of meeting you."

"As Aletha has just said, Your Grace," Miklós replied, "I have something important to say, and that is that I wish to marry your daughter!"

*　　*　　*

Aletha stood looking at the view.

She thought nothing could be more beautiful or more compelling.

The mountain on which she stood was high above the valley in which a river was glinting in the sunshine.

There was meadowland on either side of it.

Beyond was another range of mountains as high as the one on which she was standing at the moment.

Miklós's house, which was his own private retreat, was small but exquisite.

It had every possible comfort.

They had arrived late the previous night, and that

morning she had awoken to think she must have been taken up to Heaven itself.

"Have you been awake for long?" she asked when she opened her eyes.

"I found it hard to sleep," Miklós said in his deep voice, "when you were beside me and at last we were alone."

He was touching her body and a flame began to flicker in her heart.

"I thought all the festivities and good wishes would never end!" he went on. "I wanted you like this, where no one could disturb us and I could tell you how much I love you from first thing in the morning and all through the night."

Aletha laughed.

"Oh, darling, no one . . . wanted it . . . more than I did . . . but I had no idea it would be so beautiful or that I could be . . . so happy!"

It had been impossible for Prince Jözsel and the Duke to allow them to be married as quickly as Miklós wanted.

First they had gone to England, where he had met most of the Ling relatives, all of whom found him charming.

They made such a fuss of him that Aletha was half-afraid he would find somebody he loved more than her.

When they were alone she expressed her doubts.

But Miklós kissed her so demandingly that he made it very clear how much he wanted her.

He told her a thousand times how frustrating it was for them not to be married, as he had wanted, immediately.

Then at last, with what the Duke called "indecent haste" they were married in the Chapel at Ling.

Crowds of their relations had filled the great house and all the neighbours' houses as well.

After a few days Honeymoon in England they had come back to Hungary.

Prince Józsel had no intention of not celebrating their marriage at the Palace.

All the rooms were packed to bursting.

The wedding festivities included Gypsy music, besides a formal ball with the best Orchestra from Vienna.

Johann Strauss had even come himself to conduct it.

As Aletha said—could anybody ask for more?

"All I want is you to myself!" Miklós had complained.

At last they had escaped.

This morning Aletha had her first chance of seeing in the daylight how fantastic the view was from Miklós's house.

As he put his arm round her waist she said:

"Now I know I have reached Paradise."

"That is how I want you to feel, my precious darling. When I built this house I thought it was the right setting for me. Now I know it is the right setting for you. You are not a Sylph, you are an Angel—my Angel! Who will always belong to me!"

His lips were on hers.

He kissed her until she felt as if they were touching the sun and its light was burning through them.

"I love you . . . oh, Miklós . . . I love you!" she whispered.

"As I love you!" he said. "And I want to tell you how much, but you are standing precariously on top of a precipice, so I suggest we go back into the house."

She saw by the fire in his eyes what he intended and exclaimed:

"But darling . . . we have only just got up!"

"What does it matter?" he asked. "When one is in love, time stands still, and I know only that I love you, I want you, and you are mine!"

Aletha laughed.

She let him take her back to the house.

They went back into the beautiful room with a view over the valley.

It was where they had slept the previous night.

As Miklós shut the door, Aletha put out her arms towards him.

He crushed her against him and she said:

"Darling . . . darling . . . I love . . . you! But I am . . . sure there is a lot . . . more for me to . . . see outside."

"There is tomorrow and the rest of our lives in which to see it," Miklós answered. "At the moment there is only love."

He carried her to the bed.

Then he was kissing her wildly, passionately, demandingly.

She knew this was the love she had prayed for and nothing else mattered.

Position, wealth, even beauty itself could not be compared to the wonder of what they felt for each other.

Then as Miklós made her his she could hear the

music that was the beat of their hearts.

The sunlight was seeping through them like leaping flames of fire.

The light which came from God and was . . . Divine enveloped them.

Then there was nothing either in Heaven or Earth but Love.

## ABOUT THE AUTHOR

**Barbara Cartland,** the world's most famous romantic novelist, who is also an historian, playwright, lecturer, political speaker and television personality, has now written over 543 books and sold over 600 million copies all over the world.

She has also had many historical works published and has written four autobiographies as well as the biographies of her mother and that of her brother, Ronald Cartland, who was the first Member of Parliament to be killed in the last war. This book has a preface by Sir Winston Churchill and has just been republished with an introduction by Sir Arthur Bryant.

*Love at the Helm*, a novel written with the help and inspiration of the late Earl Mountbatten of Burma, Great Uncle of His Royal Highness The Prince of Wales, is being sold for the Mountbatten Memorial Trust.

She has broken the world record for the last sixteen years by writing an average of twenty-three books a year. In the *Guinness Book of Records* she is listed as the world's top-selling author.

Miss Cartland in 1978 sang an Album of Love Songs with the Royal Philharmonic Orchestra.

In private life Barbara Cartland, who is a Dame of the Order of St. John of Jerusalem, Chairman of the St. John Council in Hertfordshire and Deputy President of the St. John Ambulance Brigade, has fought for better conditions and salaries for Midwives and Nurses.

She championed the cause for the Elderly in 1956 invoking a Government Enquiry into the "Housing Conditions of Old People."

In 1962 she had the Law of England changed so that Local Authorities had to provide camps for their own Gypsies. This has meant that since then thousands and thousands of Gypsy children have been able to go to School, which they had never been able to do in the past, as their caravans were moved every twenty-four hours by the Police.

There are now fourteen camps in Hertfordshire and Barbara Cartland has her own Romany Gypsy Camp called Barbaraville by the Gypsies.

Her designs "Decorating with Love" are being sold all over the U.S.A. and the National Home Fashions League made her, in 1981, "Woman of Achievement."

She is unique in that she was one and two in the Dalton list of Best Sellers, and one week had four books in the top twenty.

Barbara Cartland's book *Getting Older, Growing*

*Younger* has been published in Great Britain and the U.S.A. and her fifth cookery book, *The Romance of Food*, is now being used by the House of Commons.

In 1984 she received at Kennedy Airport America's Bishop Wright Air Industry Award for her contribution to the development of aviation. In 1931 she and two R.A.F. Officers thought of, and carried, the first aeroplane-towed glider airmail.

During the War she was Chief Lady Welfare Officer in Bedfordshire looking after 20,000 Service men and women. She thought of having a pool of Wedding Dresses at the War Office so a Service Bride could hire a gown for the day.

She bought 1,000 gowns without coupons for the A.T.S., the W.A.A.F.'s and the W.R.E.N.S. In 1945 Barbara Cartland received the Certificate of Merit from Eastern Command.

In 1964 Barbara Cartland founded the National Association for Health of which she is the President, as a front for all the Health Stores and for any product made as alternative medicine.

This is now a £65 million turnover a year, with one third going in export.

In January 1988 she received *La Médaille de Vermeil de la Ville de Paris*. This is the highest award to be given in France by the City of Paris. She has sold 25 million books in France.

In March 1988 Barbara Cartland was asked by the Indian Government to open their Health Resort outside Delhi. This is almost the largest Health Resort in the world.

Barbara Cartland was received with great enthusiasm by her fans, who fêted her at a reception in the

City, and she received the gift of an embossed plate from the Government.

Barbara Cartland was made a Dame of the Order of the British Empire in the 1991 New Year's Honours List by Her Majesty, The Queen, for her contribution to Literature and also for her years of work for the community.